Marathon of Madness

By Christopher Woods

Dead Man's Run: Book 3

Three Ravens Publishing
Chickamauga, GA USA

Welcome to the world of the Car Warriors: Autoduel Chronicles — Tales from the freeways of the future, where the right of way goes to the biggest guns and death sports rule the airwaves. From clandestine highway battles to prime-time arena combat, jump behind the wheel, follow the fast-paced action, and never forget to Drive Offensively!

Car Warriors Autoduel fiction is licensed by Steve Jackson Games Incorporated and set in the *Car Wars* universe.

Marathon Of Madness By Christopher Woods
Published by Three Ravens Publishing
threeravenspublishing@gmail.com
P O Box 851, Chickamauga, GA 30707
https://www.threeravenspublishing.com
Copyright © 2024 by Steve Jackson Games

Publisher's Note: This is a work of fiction. Names, characters, places, and incidents are a product of the author's imagination. Locales and public names are sometimes used for atmospheric purposes. Any resemblance to actual people, living or dead, or to businesses, companies, events, institutions, or locales is completely coincidental.

Credits:
Marathon Of Madness was written by Christopher Woods
Cover art by: oldmanlogan
MARATHON OF MADNESS by: Christopher Woods /Three Ravens Publishing – 1st edition, 2024

Ebook ISBN: 978-1-962791-67-0
Trade Paperback ISBN: 978-1-962791-68-7
Audiobook ISBN: 978-1-962791-69-4

Thank you, to all of our backers of the Car Warriors
Kickstarter project!

-Jessie D. Foster
-Kevin A Davis
-David Hankins
-Alyssa Casto
-Jeffrey Riggs
-Jorge Markin
-Randal Dilday
-Julian W.
Thompson
-Jeff Dodge
-Rich Neves
-Cursed Dragon
Ship Publishing
-Stace Johnson
-Val Cassotta
-Jef Farnsworth
-Jeffery Sergent
-Jason Walters
-Mark Wagner
-Keith Unger
-Jonathan Hurley
-Jim Tullis
-Mark Strahm
-Karl J. Smith
-John Pieper
-Dustin
"TinyMonster"
Rhoades
-Jedikiah
Springfield
-Larry Southard
-Jeff Johnson
-James Emil
Conason
-Aaron Spriggs
-Scott Long
-Reed Snyder
-K.C. L'Roy
-Tee Stoney
-Todd DeWolfe
-Brian Thacker

-Caleb Pittman
-David A. Jepson
-Tad K
-David Glover
-Ramón Terrell
-Eric Stuyvesant
-Gavin Inglis
-Mark Stallings
-Brooks Moses
-Brian Healy
-KB Carlisle
-Andrew Franklin
-Stephen Dedman
-Rolf Laun
-Wild Card
-Marc Alan
Edelheit
-Rob Kamm
-Peter J. Jansen
-Nicholas D
Miller
-Danny White
-Jordan C
-Kenta
Washington
-Robert Gilson
-Marcus Evenstar
-Sammy
-Kim the
Troublemaker
-Jonathan Bowen
-Brian John
Skillen
-Jim Davenport
-Monty
Rasmussen
-Alex Rath
-Ch. N. Heinzl
-Bart Kemper
-Jim Tetrick
-Jason Lankford

-Glitz & Blam
-Eric Moorefield
-Jerry 'Archer'
Schaefer
-Milton
Fernandez
-Jim McLaughlin

Table of Contents

Chapter 1

I kept my eyes on the horizon as I took a bite of the algae burger I had packed for my lunch. My right hand stayed on my leg, close to the .50 cal on my side.

"You're not on duty, Jake," Devin Gray said from her seat across from me in the wagon.

The "wagon" was an old Budget Box pulled by an equally old Barcelona rig. She was light on firepower but that's what we were there for. The Budget was to carry the work crew and supplies for road repairs. It was cooler than the sweltering heat outside and my crew of guards were inside for lunch. I sat near the back where I could see outside and still get some of the coolness from the air conditioning.

"Always on duty, Dev."

"Lenny has us covered," she said. "You're always too worried."

"He's got reason to be, Dev," Garret Lee said from the seat beside me. "Ole Jake, here, is a 'roadkill virgin'."

"That's not all that unusual. Over half the crew are virgins."

I kept chewing my burger and watching the roads.

"Yeah, but no one here's been workin' the road crews over five years and hasn't been roadkill except Jake."

"You've been out here five years?"

I glanced toward the blonde guard. "Somewhere thereabouts."

"And you weren't hit in those five years?"

"Seven times."

"Seven raids and you weren't shot any of those times?"

"I been shot a few times."

"One time he dragged himself close to a quarter of a mile and stole one of the raider's bikes. Came draggin' in to the shop half dead."

"I'm not sure I wouldn't rather get the roadkill treatment," she said. "At least you don't have to remember the dying or dragging yourself a quarter mile. I did my Gold Cross upload just before this trip."

I looked at her again and shook my head.

"You're not one of those bible thumpers, are you, Jake? Worried about your soul?"

"Not all that religious," I said. "Just don't like the thought of dyin' and I'm gonna try to make sure it don't happen anytime soon."

"Well, if we have souls, most of us lost 'em a long time ago," Garret said. "I used to believe. Then a couple years back I got killed out on I-40. I'm back and I don't feel any different."

"You look different," I said. "Uglier than the north end of a southbound baboon, now. You were almost pretty before."

"I look the same as I did."

"That's just what they let you think," I said with my face turned away from him to hide the grin.

"No way! They're not allowed to mess with the uploads!"

"How would you even know?" I turned back to him with a serious look.

"How would I know?" He paused. "Oh my god, how would I know?"

He stood up, sandwich in hand, and moved to the front of the trailer. "Kelly! Look at me. Do I look the same as before the thing on I-40?"

She looked up from the bowl of soup she was eating. "Nah, you were a little better lookin' before."

"Gah!" He turned and passed us as he left the trailer. "Larry!"

Devin giggled. "That was just mean."

"Maybe." I chuckled. "He quit tellin' stories about me though."

"True, but now he got me curious. Seven times?"

"Yea. Those bastards down in Athens are mean. Four times they hit us over the years. Fought 'em off all four times. Lost a few guards but no crew. Fifth was out on I-40 just shy of Crossville. Barely got out of that one with my hide. They got the crew and guards on that raid. It was messy. They killed twenty-two people trying to get an old truck and a Budget Box. I don't even know what drives people like that. There's no food shortages like there were back in the days of the Food Riots. It's not like we carry a bunch of supplies or any wealth. We got a truck full of asphalt and a couple of pickups full of guards."

"What did they take?"

"They didn't take anything." I was quiet for a moment. "None of 'em survived."

"How many did you...?"

"Enough. I told you, I'm not too keen on bein' dead. Took one in the leg, another grazed me just below the ribs, but I managed to get to a bike and made it back to the shop."

"So that's five. What about the other two?"

"Same old story, different highway." I didn't want to think about the first one.

"I've only been with the company for a year. We had a skirmish with a group of bikers a couple months back on

I-40 east of Knoxville," she said. "Never been shot though."

"Well let's hope it stays that way," I said. "It ain't no fun. I'd rather the idiots shoot each other and leave the road crews alone. How do they think they get their supplies? Roads go down and most of the small towns are screwed."

"They might want the roads messed up, so the traffic is slower. Easier targets."

"Could be. Who knows with these idiots?"

I glanced down at my watch and finished the last of my burger. "Looks like it's time to get back to work."

"We still got five minutes," she said. "I'm gonna soak up a little more air conditioning before stepping back out there."

"Don't blame you," I said as I stepped out of the back of the trailer.

It was close to a hundred degrees out and body armor was hot. I picked up my rifle that was leaning against the side and held it close to my chest. If I needed the weapon, it was right in my hands.

I was almost ten feet from the trailer when I heard the high pitch of the incoming rocket. I turned back toward the trailer.

"Dev!"

I saw the rocket and had no time to do anything but cover my face with my arms before it struck the trailer. I saw the flash and felt like I was kicked by a mule. The force of the blast threw over the guard rail and I rolled down a hill into a gully. My head struck something, and I sank into blackness.

It was a different kind of blackness that I awoke to. I must have been out for hours, and night had come.

"That was the last of 'em, Dalton." The voice came from above me on the road.

I no longer held my rifle, so I carefully reached for the pistol. It was gone and my hand came back wet. I wiped the wetness on my shirt and slowly moved. No sharp pains greeted me. Just the throbbing in my head.

"They didn't have much," another voice answered. "We got lucky the other squad was in the box."

I inched my way toward the voices.

"That's where any of the good stuff was," first voice said.

"They didn't have any good stuff," second voice responded. "I keep tellin' the boss these road crews don't have anything."

"We got some new weapons."

"There is that."

I reached the guard rail. I could see the two men standing there watching the still burning trailer. Slowly, I drew the hunting knife from my waist.

"I'm gonna go see if the boss is ready to go," second voice said and moved away.

"I guess I'll just stay here and watch the fire," first voice muttered.

Then my hand slipped over his mouth and pulled his head back for my blade to do what it was intended for.

My grandad used to tell me when you're in a fight a blade is used to get a gun. A gun is used to get a bigger gun.

As the raider sank to the ground, I held his automatic in my right hand and my bloody blade in the left. A slow rage was burning in my chest as I slipped into the night after the other raider.

Two trucks full of guards pulled up to the site as dawn broke. I was staring at the charred remains of my squad in the smoldering trailer.

"Sure glad you won't remember that, Dev."

Most of the blood that covered me wasn't mine and I suppose it was a hell of a thing to drive up on. The road crew and both guard squads were dead. Fourteen raiders were scattered among the bodies and five more were down the road beside their transport.

"Jake?"

"I'm still here, boss," I said.

Phil Clayton stopped in front of me. "You get 'em all?"

"Second squad got some of them."

"First squad?"

I pointed at the trailer.

"Jesus."

"I don't think Jesus had anything to do with this."

"Go to the truck, Jake. Let Terri take a look at you."

I nodded and walked toward the truck. My feet were heavy and my eyes drooped. I was tired. So tired.

Chapter 2

I sat down in the lobby, making sure to pick one of the benches which left my right side unhindered. It was a force of habit to keep my gun free of obstacles. I'd found my .50 cal after the fight, and it rested against my hip.

I remembered someone saying an armed society was a polite society. I was pretty sure they hadn't lived in east Tennessee. There was little politeness outside of the city. Other places called Tennessee the lawless lands and they were fairly accurate. We pretty much governed ourselves except for the cities which were run by the corporations, and they'd fortified them pretty heavily.

"They'll see you now, Mister Turner."

I looked up to find a blonde woman peeking out of a door on my left.

"Ma'am," I said with a nod and followed her inside the door to a long hallway.

The TTA building was large, and I had only been in the corporate headquarters once. Most of my dealings with the Tennessee Titan Authority had been in the local road crew shop until now.

We stopped at a security station.

"You'll need to check your weapons here sir," the guide said.

"That's new," I said.

"Management security, sir."

"It's Jake," I said.

She held the drawer open, and I placed the hand cannon inside along with four blades of various types.

She was looking at me with an eyebrow raised.

I shrugged. "Sometimes you need a knife."

"The scanner says there's another in your boot."

"Heh, almost forgot about that one."

I drew the toothpick from the sheath inside my left boot and placed it in the drawer with the others.

"Any idea why management wants to speak with me?"

"No, sir … Jake."

"Probably couldn't tell me if you did," I said. "Lead on, ma'am."

There was a worried look on her face that she couldn't quite mask, although she tried.

I started feeling it myself.

She led me down another hall, deeper into headquarters. After a few minutes she motioned to a door. "They're waiting inside."

I nodded and opened the door.

Inside was a bare room with a long table on the far side. Behind the table sat three people. One was a very attractive brunette woman in a black business suit. Her blouse was unbuttoned far enough to distract most men, but her eyes were ice cold. To her left was a man about forty or so years old with some greying at the temple. His black suit was immaculate, and he looked at me with pale blue eyes. There was still more warmth in his eyes than the brunette. The last one was a guy in a rumpled suit wearing focals, eyewear designed to be used as a computer interface.

"Mister Turner," grey man said. "Please have a seat."

I nodded and sat in the single chair on my side of the table.

"Do you know why you're here, Mister Turner?"

"I assume it's about the raid last month."

"Indeed." Grey man turned to the others. "This is Hannah Forth, our head of Human Resources. And this is Nigel Trent. Nigel specializes in probabilities, percentages … he's a number guy. I'm Frank Keller, Road Division Manager of TTA."

"What can I do for you, then?"

"When Nigel comes to me with his statistics, most of the time my eyes glaze over and I have a hard time with them, but this time he starts talking about a guy that's come back as the sole survivor of, not just one, but three raids over the last five years. When we see numbers like that, we have to look into it."

"I can understand that," I said. "But I'm not sure what you want me to say."

"Just tell us what happened."

"They used a rocket that took out the Box while my squad was inside for lunch. The blast threw me over the rail and down in a gully. Hit my head and missed most of the rest. When I came to, they were looting my friends' bodies and having a good ole time."

"Then what happened?"

"You've read the reports."

"I have but I need to hear it from you."

"It didn't sit right with me, them having their own little party on my friends' ashes, so I killed 'em."

"How many?"

"Listen," I said. "All of this is in the report. I'm not exactly proud of it but I have some skill at it, and everything's been gone over again and again."

"Answer the question," Forth said. Her voice was as cold as her eyes.

"Fifteen, alright?" I scowled. "I killed fifteen men out there. Do you want every bloody detail?"

She looked at Nigel who nodded.

"The reason we needed you here is to see if Nigel's numbers were accurate," Keller said. "There are a number of sensors recording you in every possible way to tell us if you are lying, Mister Turner. He says you've been telling the truth."

He turned to the others. "You may leave."

Forth and Trent stood and exited the door behind them. Forth was scowling as she turned away.

"Nigel's probabilities pointed toward you being aligned with the raiders. It seems the probabilities don't take into account the person who is in the position. What happens next is that I write up the report of what I believe and send it up the chain. For what it's worth, I think your claims are accurate and you are just a very difficult man to kill. TTA deals a great deal in numbers, though, Mister Turner, and I'm afraid it's going to come down to Human Resources and numbers."

"You're gonna drop me, right?"

"It will be up to the company, but I'll give them my recommendation."

I let out a long slow breath. "I guess I can get another job."

"You don't understand, son. If they go with the numbers, they say you're a raider and a killer. You won't find work in Knoxville with that hanging over your head."

"What?"

"Best of luck, kid," he said. "If it goes badly, I'll still reference you in another city."

He stood up and walked out the door.

I sat there for a full minute.

"What the hell?" I muttered as I stood up.

The blonde was still outside the door but there were two large men with her.

I nodded and chuckled. "You ain't got to worry about me, boys. I've already reached my quota on fightin' for the month."

They still hovered at my shoulders as the blonde led me back out of the building.

We walked past the security station where I'd left my stuff. "Your weapons will be returned as you exit, sir."

"Reckon they already decided."

Chapter 3

With my weapons back in their former places, I walked down to the street from the TTA building. They didn't send drones out with us on the road crews. All they had was my word and the bodies to prove me right or wrong. None of the vehicles or weapons had been taken from the site so it seemed like they would have listened to the report.

I raised my hand as I saw the bus approaching. I was still dazed as I sat down in the rear seat. I guess I wasn't looking too friendly, and no one bothered to talk to me on the trip out to the outskirts where the Road Department was located.

I guess it was understandable. I'm a pretty big guy with long hair and a beard. Six feet three inches tall and I guess you might say I was pretty scruffy. The scowl I was carrying was probably enough to keep folks from wanting to interact with me.

Soon enough, the bus stopped in front of the shop, and I exited. I wasn't sure where to go. They hadn't officially fired me yet, but I knew what was coming. Keller had told me as much.

I turned as one of the crew trucks pulled in and knew where I should go. If the Gold Cross upload was still active, I should use it before the news came down. Even if I lost the perk as an employee, they would keep the upload indefinitely. It would just go in a databank somewhere.

I watched the passengers unload from the truck. They were fresh from the tanks at Gold Cross where they had been downloaded into their clones. They had that confused look on their faces as they began adjusting to the new bodies. All of them were pale and their skin was unblemished.

"Glad you won't remember what happened," I muttered as Dev stepped down from the trailer. I turned and flagged an incoming bus.

Gold Cross was unmistakable with the huge golden cross on the front of the massive building. When we signed on with the road crews, we all were brought here for them to get samples of our DNA so they could have a clone in reserve for us. They specialized in neuroscience, and they had developed the technology to copy a person's mind and store it on a databank. If the worst happened, you or a version of you could be placed in a clone and you were as good as new.

A lot of religious types declared it an abomination to copy yourself into another body and called those who had been downloaded soulless. I didn't know whether they were right or not, but if I died there would be a version of me in that databank.

They were only allowed to have a single copy of any one person in the databanks at any given time. I assumed there were multiples for a short time as the systems connected and updated the main storage facility. But it was a very short time.

Road crews updated before every job just in case. It wasn't normal for one of us to upload directly after a job, but this might be the last upload I would get to do. I figured I'd like the most current version I could get.

The first thing I saw when entering the lobby was the bold print behind the receptionist.

Out of darkness, we bring light.

Thank you for trusting Gold Cross with all of your rebirth needs.

Don't forget to ask an associate about our monthly premium renewal specials.

My eyes dropped from the print on the wall, and I recognized the girl at the front desk from the upload I did just before heading out to the job.

"Rebecca, isn't it?" I said as I stopped in front of the desk.

Her focals flashed as she looked up. "Mister Turner."

I chuckled. "That's cheating."

She grinned. "It's an automatic setting on the focals. If it helps, I remember you from last month. I didn't think they were sending any crews out for a little while after that one."

"They're not. I'm heading home to Tazewell for a little while and thought I'd see if I can refresh the upload before I go."

She cocked her head to the side a fraction as she checked. The focals flashed again as data crossed the screen. "I don't see why not. We have a tech available right now if you want to go ahead."

"Great! I usually have a wait."

"We downloaded quite a few this morning so we have techs aplenty. Did you hear? A whole road crew was wiped out by Raiders down in Sweetwater. They said there was only one surv…" Her focals were still cycling data. "Oh my, that was your crew?"

I nodded.

"That's horrible," she said. "If only they could, I would want to have them load the last upload into me after something like that."

"Don't think the thought didn't cross my mind," I said. "But the rules are the rules."

"How bad was it?"

"Bad enough," I said. "I'd like to forget it, but it doesn't work that way."

"Are you sure you don't want to keep the other one just in case?"

"I guess I need to keep the one in my head. I'll have to update some time anyway."

"True. If you go down to room 51, Janice will help you."

"Thanks." I turned to my left and entered the hallway that circled the outside of the building.

The thought of copying last week's me over current me was an appealing thought but it wouldn't help TTA change their minds, whatever decision they made.

I entered room 51 to find a young man waiting.

"I'm supposed to see Janice," I said.

"That's me," he said with a grin. "I love to see that reaction. That's why I kept the name. Technically, I'm Janice two point oh."

"Heh. How's that work?"

"Back, umpteen years ago I got a medical procedure. I was young and dumb. When I did use my Gold Cross, I came back as my original. DNA is DNA."

"I guess so."

"Are you ready for your upload?"

"Ready as I'll ever be."

I watched Janice approach the console and motioned for me to lie on the table in front of the round opening. I hated when they slid me into the hole. I'm a big guy and it's uncomfortable.

I knew several people like Janice who switched from male to female or the other way around. If you want to try living life as the other sex, who was I to judge? Just be prepared to have to do it again if you ever do the Gold Cross thing.

"Reckon God can sort it all out," I muttered.

"Now that's something I don't hear very often."

I chuckled. "I guess not. I guess religion's kind of the opposite of this place."

"Depends on how you look at it, Mister Turner. I prefer to believe that my soul moves with my consciousness. Once my consciousness enters this body the soul does as well."

"Makes sense," I said and shrugged. "I don't have a clue how it works."

"That's where faith comes in, Mister Turner."

"I reckon so."

The table slid into the hole with bare inches on each side of my shoulders. I swallowed as the space around me got cramped.

I guess he could be right about the soul. I tried not to worry too much about it anyway. If there was a Heaven and Hell, I figured I knew which one I was slated for. Once you kill a bunch of folks, I don't know if you get to go to Heaven. I'll leave that up to the judge at the end. Until then I would try my best to stay alive.

After quite some time, the table slid out of the tube, and I was greeted by an unsmiling tech.

"Were you aware of the fact that TTA would rescind any use of our services today?"

"I figured there was a good chance of it. Hoped I could get a current upload into the system before they did."

"Do you know what they are accusing you of?"

"I'm aware." I nodded. "They're wrong."

He pressed a button on the console. "You are updated, Mister Turner. If there is ever any pursuit of the charges they have accused you of, the courts will have to make those decisions. I like to go on my first impression when dealing with people, and it's usually pretty accurate."

"Thank you."

"Oh, no," he said in a higher pitch, cycling through a message on his focal. "I just received notice your updating privileges are revoked. Please leave the premises, Mister Turner."

I nodded and walked out of the room.

Chapter 4

In all likelihood, they would just blackball me from getting work in Knoxville with rumors. There would be no charges... officially. I couldn't afford to clear my name on my own, so I was going to have to leave. Hard to win a fight when you're unarmed. TTA was well armed, having money to spare.

I came to Knoxville five and a half years ago to make money. I squirreled away every penny I could, but lawyers cost a lot of money. More than I had, that's for sure.

I exited the bus once again at the shop.

As I walked across the lot toward the office, I saw a pair of guards head my direction. It wasn't hard to recognize both of them. I had been eating lunch with them just before they were killed.

Garrett stopped in front of me with a scowl.

"Is it true?" Devin asked.

"Which part?" I asked in return. "Did I survive another raid? Yes. Am I working with raiders? No."

"I couldn't believe it when they told us what the company's saying." Garrett was visibly relieved. "You killed the bastards?"

"I did. Every damn one of them."

He nodded and turned away.

"Simple as that?" Devin asked.

"He looked us in the eye and talked straight, Dev."

"Believe me or not, Dev," I said. "Either way they've seen to it I'm done here. I'm getting my things and going back home."

"What if some of us don't believe you? What if we decided to return the favor, instead?"

"You've worked with me on four jobs, Dev. Do what you have to. But if anyone draws down on me today it's gonna get real ugly real fast. Now I'm pretty slow to anger, but the company I've sweated and bled for over the last five years just shit canned me because of a bunch of statistics from a guy that's been sitting in their tower all of his life. His numbers don't account for me. You guys are the ones I've worked with over that five years. I like you Dev and I'll probably never be able to scrub your death from the things I've seen. I killed fifteen men because of what I saw. I could have snuck off into the woods and waited for our people to get there, but they killed my friends."

She stepped back a step at the fury in my words.

"Now they're turning the very friends I avenged against me. Wouldn't that just be the hardest twist from this knife in my back?"

"There's been talk," Garrett said.

"I expect so. Garrett, you and Dev go tell 'em I'm picking up my stuff and leaving. Not sure if TTA is gonna give 'em another clone body if they pick a fight here in town."

"You're that sure of yourself?" Dev asked. "There's a whole squad here on duty."

"Honestly, Dev? I am. Now I'm cleaning out my locker and getting my bike. It's been a pleasure workin' with you guys."

I turned my back on them and walked into the office where Phil Clayton was waiting.

"That was a little tense, Jake."

"You gonna grill me too?"

"Nope, I took your report and saw the scene. If you'd been working with them, you wouldn't have killed them all. Still have to give you the 'official' pink slip."

"I expect so."

"They followed their contract and sent your severance package."

"I didn't expect that."

"I reckon if they didn't, you'd have to be 'officially' declared a criminal and charged."

"Seems like they'd want the truth."

"Truth doesn't play into the actions of the company very much, Jake. We all know that." He motioned toward the door I had come in. "They'll realize that soon enough. They're all fresh out of the vat and still processing what happened. I'm going to go over the report with them today, so I suspect you'll have no trouble with them."

"I hope not," I said. "Been good workin' for you, boss."

"You're one of the best, Jake, and what you've done on three occasions that I've seen is scary. You ever thought of channeling that into something else? Maybe try Deathball or, damn, you'd be a hell of a gunner in the arena."

"Paid to die over and over? I've been tryin' my level best not to die. Not sure I want to go out and do it for the masses."

"Yeah, but there's a lot of money in it."

"Nah, I'll go back to the hills and make shine. It's not the business it used to be, but it still pays."

"Nowhere near what this does and definitely nowhere near the autoduels."

"Not sure if I wanna go that route," I said.

"They got something big coming. They been talking about a long distance thing. They want to raise the ratings."

"I don't doubt that," I said. "People get tired of watchin' the same people kill each other over and over."

"Amateur Night has the highest ratings of any show every month."

"You watch too much TV, boss."

"I probably do." He rested a hand on my shoulder. "Your Spider's prepped and ready to go. I gave you a full load out on the weapons."

I raised an eyebrow.

"I was guessing you'd be heading home. If you're running through Maynardville, I figured you better have a full load."

"Thanks, boss."

"Just Phil, now."

"Thanks, Phil."

"Try not to get yourself killed out there, Jake."

I nodded, slipped the envelope with my termination papers and severance package into my jacket, and walked out the door.

Chapter 5

Phil was true to his word. The Spider I took from the raiders out on I40 was in the bay beside the office. I checked the ammo boxes for the two mini guns to find them topped off. He'd even loaded the twin rocket launchers on the rear. They were a pursuit deterrent. Hard to aim behind you, but if someone got too close, the rockets were good for stopping them.

I put the helmet on which had links to the weapon targeting system. It was the nicest bike the raiders had brought when they hit the road crew and none of them could use it, or anything else, for that matter. Being the sole survivor, salvage rights made the thing mine. I filed the rights as soon as I recovered from the wounds I took during the fight.

I shook my head as I drove out of the garage. There was a group of people in the parking lot who watched my departure. A few of them waved but I couldn't shake the scowling look that I saw on Dev's face. It was on several of the others. They'd believe the company over me, and I couldn't say if they were wrong. Loyalty was pretty important when you were putting your life on the line for someone. It's sad when they don't deserve that loyalty, though.

I wasn't too worried about any of them trying to take a shot at me as long as they were out in the lot. I did worry about someone who could be hiding with a rifle. As soon as my tires hit the pavement, I jammed the throttle and shot forward. The sensors on the helmet didn't detect any shots and I cut back on the throttle after rounding the bend on Dannaher Drive which would take me out to Emory Road. There was a National Commerce Bank on Emory where I could deposit the pay from the severance package.

NCB was an AADA sanctioned finance company that I know would be honored nationwide. Even out in the "lawless" areas. The smaller branches they had in Maynardville and Tazewell didn't keep large amounts of cash on hand but most banking was done digitally anyway.

I smiled up at the camera mounted beside the mini gun turret as I stopped in the drive through and slipped my credit stick into the tube. Pressing the button to send it to the teller, I looked again at the turret.

Pop used to tell me about the old days when they didn't have armed drive-thrus at the banks. He was a kid, but he remembered when you didn't have to go armed everywhere you traveled. Before the Bad Times.

"Deposit?" the female voice on the speaker asked.

"Yes."

"Done," she said. "Is there anything else I can do for you?"

"Nope, that should do it."

"Have a nice day, Mister Turner."

"You too," I said.

I throttled the Spider and turned right on Emory Road. It was still a couple of miles to the wall. After I exited, I would have to be a lot more wary. These wouldn't be interstate roads and the repair would be spotty at best. The good thing was the Spider had a heavy suspension and could be used off road if needed.

I didn't expect trouble until I reached Maynardville, and it was a fifty-fifty chance even there. Despite what the vids spewed, it wasn't a full time shootout when you left the cities. Even on the crews, we only got hit maybe once a year and they knew where we were going to be.

I waved at the guards on the checkpoint out of the city as I drove through the gate. There was almost no traffic going north and several vehicles lined up to enter the gates. Three of them were pickups loaded with salvage to sell at the markets. It would be great to bring in vegetables if you could grow any. You'd get one hell of a payday if you could manage that. Algae was the prime source of food and there was no lack of it but corn and beans would fetch an insane price if you manage to grow it.

Larry always said it wasn't worth the time you had to spend guarding it. Making liquor was a lot easier. I was pretty sure he just didn't want to put in the work of growing it. He bought his corn from Trip Hopper. Trip had enough kids that guard duty on his grow vaults wasn't a problem.

I used the helmet to scan the roads ahead and throttled up the Spider. The biggest worry I had was a lone hunter out in the hills who happened to be in the right place at the right time. Or if Maynardville had lookouts set up to warn them of an approaching vehicle. I could bypass Maynardville by using Hickory Valley Road but that had its own issues. The Flatfords were a hard-assed bunch that had taken over there and I would have to go through their territory. Better to deal with Maynardville than the Flatfords.

As I topped Copper Ridge, I saw an old Haymaker in the other lane heading toward Knoxville. I saw brake lights just as I dropped down the other side.

Grinning, I throttled the Spider. No way was a Haymaker catching a Spider. The only worry was whether they called anyone in Maynardville. Engaging long range sensors to scan the highway ahead, I had a pretty good solution for that.

The bike shot forward as I throttled her up. The sensors laid a grid in my visor over the road ahead and highlighted the rough patches with red. There was a slim track of green and I only slowed marginally for curves. The Spider was nice considering where I had acquired it. Raiders didn't usually have that good of equipment. It was a hell of a find.

Sensors picked up several vehicles approaching Maynardville Highway from side roads and I laughed as I blew past them at a hundred miles per hour. They were still setting up their roadblock at the edge of town when I passed them. There were a few shots, but nothing came close. They had expected ten or fifteen minutes before I rode in. There would have definitely been a tax to pass the block. Worse when they found out I was from Tazewell. Most times it was a beating, sometimes it was a bit more permanent.

I wasn't sure where all the animosity came from, but the feud had been going on as long as I could remember. Only place I knew where Tazewell and Maynardville folks remained peaceful was Sharp's Chapel, which was nestled right between them.

Sharp's Chapel held the bridge, and it was the only way across the lake without going around by way of Morristown. And they didn't give one damn whether they blew it up or left it open. They declared the Chapel neutral ground and enforced it pretty harshly.

A bunch of fellas from Maynardville thought they would ride into the Chapel and set them straight. No one ever saw those boys again. I reckoned they were somewhere at the bottom of Norris Lake.

I waved at the group on the other side of town as I streaked past and flew up Maynardville Ridge, going airborne as I crossed the summit. Sparks flew and something rattled before dropping off the bottom of the Spider. I winced as I saw something bounce twice and fly into the woodland on the side of the road.

"Got a little carried away," I muttered and dropped my speed a little.

A red light flashed in my helmet as I took the curve at the bottom.

"Damn generator," I said and dropped my acceleration to save the power plant.

The generator kept the power plant charged as long as the bike was moving at regular speeds. High acceleration would drain it quicker than the generator could charge. The fact that the generator was several miles back and at the bottom of a ravine made it worse. High acceleration would drain the power plant that much quicker.

It was beginning to get dark as well and lights wouldn't help the matter. The scanners were good enough that I trusted in the tech and left the lights off. My rear viewer showed lights moving in the hills behind me. It looked like they were a little pissed and decided to follow me.

"Crap."

I thumbed the throttle again. I couldn't afford to get caught after blowing through town like that. I tripped the switch to arm the rockets in the back. If they got too close before I reached the bridge, they'd have problems.

The bike was down to fifty percent as I rolled to a stop at the bridge access point. My pursuers stopped at the top of the ridge before the bridge. They wouldn't try to tackle the defenses on the bridge. There were four turrets with fifties trained on me as I removed my helmet.

"I'll be damned," a female voice said. "Jake?"

"Hi Jackie." I grinned. "I was just about to call you. What are you doing out here?"

"My turn with the guard this month."

"Does that leave you with any time to do any greaser work?"

"Hell no." She stepped out of the shadows, looking up the road. "You making friends again?"

"Unreasonable people make life so difficult."

"Looks like Tolliver's rig," she said.

"They weren't happy about me coming through town."

"Not surprised. How fast were you moving? Seventy-five?"

"Umm… little bit faster."

"Crazy bastard," she said. "That Spider got the sensor package?"

"Yeah, it does."

There were yells from the top of the ridge.

"Come on through before those idiots decide to take a pot shot and piss off the turrets."

I barely pushed the throttle and drove through the opening gates, following Jackie.

Jackie Shoffner was probably the best Greaser I knew. She had been turning wrenches her whole life just like her father and her grandfather who she was named after.

She wasn't painful to look at either. Long black hair and vibrant grey eyes that a fella could get lost in. She was only five feet tall but there was nothing petite about the rifle she carried. I knew she was a crack shot with it too.

"Sure you don't have time to do a little wrenching? Lost my generator on Maynardville Ridge."

"Jumped it again, didn't you?"

"Maybe."

She shook her head. "I'll see if Andy can take my shift tomorrow. If he can, I'll grab a genny off one of the bikes in the yard."

"That would be great."

"You got enough charge in the power plant to get home?"

"If I don't need to throttle too much."

"Just stay at the house," she said. "We'll get a new genny on it and charge the plant up. Don't even look at me like that."

"I know, I know. We drive for the same team. A fella can dream, can't he?"

She laughed. "Keep dreaming, Jake. If I ever decide to switch, I might let you know."

"Might?"

She shrugged. "Maybe but that's even pushing it. You remember how to get there. Don't let J.J. chew on you too much."

"He's got to be getting' a little long in the tooth."

"He's old. He'll be happy to see you though. He always liked you, I'm not sure why."

"Dogs can read people." I grinned. "Doesn't hurt that I gave him jerky."

"That sounds about right." She paused. "I'm off in about an hour if you want to give me a ride instead of Dallas. It'll save him a trip up the ridge."

I nodded and put the stand down. She returned to her post out by the gate, and I stood looking out from the bridge over the lake. There were a few lights on the water where people were night fishing.

Sometimes I missed living in the hills. It looked like I would get plenty of it now though. The Company burned me pretty good in Knoxville. The nearest place I could get work that paid that well was Memphis or Chattanooga and TTA was the big dog there too. I could go east and get something in North Carolina if they didn't dig too deep into my background. It would be difficult to get work anywhere with this thing hanging over my head. It would have been a lot easier if they had brought official charges instead of just making me unhirable.

They needed a fall guy for the loss of another crew, and I was perfect. At least that was my theory. It was a pretty crappy thing to do to a guy, but Company politics are what they are. I could possibly clear my name, but it would take more money than I had.

Chapter 6

I woke up the next morning with a warm body against my side. I was pretty sure it wasn't who I wanted there since I smelled dog.

"Mornin' J.J." I petted the old Shepherd's head. He leaned into me. "I know, it's too early by far."

"Traitorous animal," Jackie said as she walked across the living room in next to nothing.

She stopped with a crooked grin on her face.

"Special torture," I said. "Tease."

She shrugged and opened the refrigerator. "Teach you to steal my dog."

"You can have him back. He smells pretty bad."

"I know. He needs a bath." She walked back through the living room to stop at the beginning of the hall. "Ginger know you're back?"

My eyes raised from where they were aimed to Jackie's face. "No one knows I'm back. Don't know that she would even care."

"What? You broke that girl's heart when you took off like that."

"Broke her heart? She dumped me right out of the blue. What was I supposed to do? Spend my days watching the girl I love runnin' round with someone else?"

"There ain't never been no one else for Ginger, you dumb ox."

"Then why'd she break things off with me?"

Jackie's mouth dropped open. "Oh my god, she didn't even tell you."

"Tell me what?"

"Jesus, Jake. I been thinkin' you did her wrong all this time by disappearin', but she didn't tell you."

My mind was racing through situations. "Was she pregnant? I don't see why that would be a problem."

"She didn't tell you." She shook her head. "No… no… no, you dumb assed girl."

I sat up. "What the hell are you saying?"

"Six years ago, just before you left, she found out she had early stage Lou Gehrig's disease."

"Lou Gehrig's? ALS?"

"All this time I never could figure why you left. I knew she broke it off, but I thought she would have told you why."

"I never would have gone if she had."

"It explains so much." She sighed. "Ginger may be the best driver I ever saw but she's a dumbass."

I was trying to process a whole lot of emotions I had buried years ago and sat there in a daze for a little while. Why would she hide something like that from me?

I was still sitting there when Jackie returned from the back of the trailer fully dressed in her coveralls.

"Well get your ass up and we'll fix the Spider. I need to ride to Tazewell, now. Gonna give her a piece of my mind."

"I'm not sure I'm ready to see her yet," I said as I stood up.

"Where the hell did you get all those?" she asked as she saw the scars all over my torso. "What have you been doin'?"

I glanced down at the old scars, remembering the night I got most of them. "Been workin' as a guard on a road crew the last five years."

"Jesus, Jake. The life expectancy of a road crew guard is two years at best. They say it's one of the most dangerous jobs."

"Road worker is worse," I said. "They aren't even combatants."

She looked closer at me.

"No, I ain't been cloned," I said. "I have an upload in the system but never had to be downloaded."

"Five years on the road crew?" She placed a hand on my chest where the long, ragged scar from my first assignment crossed from the left pec to my right rib about half way down my torso.

I shrugged. "First trip out."

"What happened?"

"Don't want to talk about it."

She stared at me for close to a minute.

I sighed. "Captured by some nasty bastards outside of Cookeville. They liked to torture their victims, knowing they'll get dropped back into a clone. I guess they figured they could do what they wanted since I would never remember it. They spent some time on me before I got loose."

"They tortured you?"

"They paid for it in spades. Learned I'm pretty good at killin'. I spent some time on them too."

"You tortured them?" her hand dropped from my chest.

"No, I just killed 'em. They won't be torturing anyone else. I doubt any of them had the use of Gold Cross."

"How many?" She was looking at me with wide eyes.

"How many people have I killed? That's the question I hear pretty often. You don't want to know the answer to that one, Jackie."

"So why are you back, Jake?"

"TTA needed a fall guy for another lost crew, and I was the best candidate."

"How's that?"

"Sole survivor. They pinned it on me, sayin' I was workin' with the raiders. Blackballed me in Knoxville so I got no work. Figured I'd run some shine with Pop."

"I don't think I could ever see you working as a raider. Too much of that hero complex for that."

"I ain't no hero."

"Bullshit," she said. "Long as I can remember you were scrappin' with the boys in town. Always because you stepped in to protect someone else."

"Heroes don't do what I've done."

"You can try to convince yourself of that, but I know better." She slapped my shoulder. "Now get dressed so we can get the Spider patched up. You're making me think of switching teams standing there in your skivvies."

"Well, now…"

"You wouldn't be thinkin' of takin' advantage of a poor girl. We all know chicks dig scars and it would ruin my whole dynamic, switchin' sides."

I chuckled and grabbed my pants from the arm of the pullout bed. "Serve you right after runnin' round the house naked this mornin'."

"I was not naked."

"If you can call that underwear clothes."

She shrugged and grinned. "It's good to see you again, Jake."

"You too, Jackie. The rest of it, I'm not sure about yet. Never really planned to come back."

"Well there's a lot of unfinished business here."

"Indeed."

Chapter 7

"You'll need this," Jackie said, handing me a navy blue scarf. "Lately we been flying one of these if we don't want to get hassled by any of the guys watching for interlopers."

"Gettin' many of those?"

"They've had a few trying to raid some of the vaults outside of town for sellable stuff. Fresh produce is still in high demand." She shrugged. "Algae can be made into a lot of things, but you can't beat a fresh cantaloupe or watermelon. You can get top dollar for those."

"I imagine."

"They caught a couple of guys cuttin' Yarby Keck's tobacco down and throwin' it in a pickup a couple months ago."

"Maynardville bunch?"

"These were out of Bean Station."

"Never had much trouble from there before. Morristown Regulators kept them in line."

"Regulators have their hands full with the Jeffersons. They been feudin' for the last two years."

"What happened to cause that?" I asked. "They been allies for years."

"Remember Billie Kates?"

"Hard to forget Billie. She's on her way to the top after that break she got with that commercial."

"She ain't anymore," she said. "Fella up in Morristown got all stalky on her and cornered her in a little joint in Jefferson City. She wasn't the same afterwards and ended up killin' herself. Bunch of Jeffersons dragged the guy out of the jail where the Regulators had him and strung him up. They killed three Regulators in the process and things went downhill ever since."

"They should have let the Regulators do their job," I said. "They ain't never been known to go easy on things like that."

"You know how people obsess about celebrities. The Regulators weren't moving fast enough for 'em."

"Damn fools," I said. "Now the whole area's in an uproar."

"You could probably get on with them if you're lookin' for work."

"TTA has a lot of pull in Morristown, seein' as it's right on the edge of the lawless lands. Any job there is gonna be shit for me, too."

She shook her head. "Corporate nonsense."

"Yup."

"Just show that scarf if anyone looks at you and you'll be fine. If you're interested, the Bulldogs might be an option."

"I got a lot of history with them, so it's doubtful. Not sure I want to be a cop anyway."

"Chapel Guard might be an option too. They don't give one damn about corporate bullshit. Pay is crap though." She laughed. "I'd put you to work in the shop, but you suck as a greaser."

"True enough. I can break it but never been much good at fixin' it afterward."

She stepped in close and hugged me. "Just be careful and go see Ginger. She has a lot to answer for after this."

I grunted. "She did what she thought was best for me. I should have dug deeper before I gave up."

I could see plain as day why she did what she did after knowing about the ALS. I wasn't sure I would have done any different. She didn't want me to have to take care of her as her nerves degenerated. ALS is a nasty bitch of a disease. You're trapped in a failing body.

If I'd known, we could have tried to figure something out. Maybe gone to the road crews together where she could get a Gold Cross upload. I'm not sure we would have even thought of that with the religious upbringing we both had. I wasn't sure about where my soul resided. I did my level best not to get killed but I didn't have a firm belief in what happened when I died.

I never saw Garrett any differently than I did before he was downloaded into a clone. He was still the same guy I had known for years, just a little softer since the clone was fresh. After a couple years, I couldn't tell him from his previous self at all. There was more difference in some because all clones were grown to about the equivalent of twenty-five years old. A fifty-year-old man could get a new lease on life.

"It's not fair," she said.

"Life ain't fair, most days."

She stepped back and I felt a little disappointment. Being close to someone I cared about was something I missed. I never got too close to anyone on the road crews because I might have to watch them die. My first assignment taught me that. I wasn't the only one they captured alive. I found the others after I broke free.

I never got overly close to them after seeing what the raiders had done to them. They were luckier than I on some levels. They would never remember those three days and I would never forget them. Too late to forget now.

I turned and pulled the helmet from the seat and put it on.

What drives people to do that kind of shit?

I wasn't sure if I would ever understand that. Sure, I understood the want to take from the haves when you're a have not. But no one was going hungry. There was enough for everyone. Basic needs weren't a problem anymore. It was rough during the Bad Times, but now, even in the Lawless Lands, people had enough to get by.

"I'll bring some of that shine back down here when I come back," I said.

"You better. Bring several cases and I'll get it sold right quick. Nobody makes as good as your grandpa around here."

"He learned how to make it from an old moonshiner in Lone Mountain."

"My Grandpa used to talk about old Bill's shine. Said it was the best around."

I nodded. "See ya later, Jackie. Take care of that old dog."

"That rotten ass thing gets whatever he wants. He's my protector, now. Old Jake Junior."

I grinned. "You ain't needed protectin' since you learned to shoot."

She patted the hand cannon resting in the holster on her hip. "True enough. Now, go see Ginger."

I grunted, thumbed the throttle on the Spider, and rolled down the hill toward Sharps Chapel Road. As I reached the bottom of the hollow, I waved at Jimmy Weaver who was just backing in a truck full of logs at the sawmill.

The Weavers had been there for as long as I remembered. They had been on that piece of property close to a hundred years. It had been close when the plagues went through. Jimmy lost everybody. He was the only Weaver to survive but he remarried and had seven kids when I left six years ago. Probably had six more by now. He waved back.

That's what I liked about the Chapel. They wave even when they have no idea who it is. His other hand was probably resting on a rifle or pistol, though. I kind of like that about the Chapel, too.

Chapter 8

I waved at the Chapel guards as I drove through the gate just before Lone Mountain Road. It was one of the checkpoints between what New Tazewell controlled and what Sharp's Chapel held. There were quite a few smaller checkpoints on the back roads that connected them as well. A lot of those roads were almost impossible to navigate though. Highway 33 was kept up pretty good, all things considered. Lone Mountain Road was pretty decent as well and it connected with 25 between Tazewell and Bean Station. Some folks preferred to avoid the town altogether.

Pop lived about halfway down Lone Mountain Road, so I took a right soon after leaving the gates. I kept the Spider at a leisurely speed driving down the two-lane. It was curvy and there were some steep spots and a couple of hairpin turns.

I was about five miles from my grandpa's place when I passed an old Galahad with a couple of guys in it. My guess was they were at one of the pull overs watching for more of those guys from Bean Station. A Galahad's a stout truck with heavy armor and decent weapon package. This one was older but looked like it was still packing some heat.

I saw the driver pull his visor down on his helmet, so I waved the blue scarf at them. He raised the visor and gave me a slight nod as I rolled past. It wasn't too much longer before I pulled in at the gate of my grandpa's place. The gate was a regular cattle gate, but the fence was six feet tall, and metal reinforced. The fence ran all the way down the five hundred feet of road frontage and back toward the rear of the property.

I stopped at the metal post with a security pad and pressed the call button.

"If you're sellin' somethin' I ain't interested."

I chuckled and removed the helmet, looking into the camera.

"I'll be damned." The gate buzzed and slid open.

I thumbed the throttle and drove inside. Pop was standing on the porch when I got down the drive and parked beside his old Conestoga.

The old station wagon looked beat up and on its last leg, but I knew what was inside of the beast. Pop used the armored station wagon to haul whiskey all over the local area. In the early days some randos from Rogersville tried to jack him as he crossed Clinch Mountain. Those boys ended up as flaming wreckage at the bottom of a ravine. Most folks recognized the wagon now and tiptoed by without waking the dragon.

I stepped off the bike and placed the helmet in the seat.

"Didn't reckon I'd ever see you again when you headed out, kid." He stepped stiffly down the step favoring his right leg. "But I'm damn glad I was wrong. How the hell are ya?"

"Been better," I said. "Glad to see you, though. What happened to your leg?"

"That damn mule kicked me."

"You still got that mean son of a bitch?"

"Nope. I ate that bastard this winter after he kicked my knee out."

I chuckled. "You been threatening to eat him ever since you got him."

"Well, I finally did it. Most of him anyway. Got a few steaks left in the freezer if you got a hankerin' for one."

"I'd love one. I'd eat it just for spite. He hated me and I wasn't too fond of him either."

He stepped up with a big grin and hugged me. "Come on in, kid. That's a nice bike."

"Not too shabby." I followed him inside.

"You must be makin' some good money out in Knoxville."

"I was."

"Was?"

"Ran into some trouble."

"Tell me." He pointed at a chair in the living room.

"You still got that chair?"

"Been there ever since you left. It's been waitin' for your ass to come back and sit in it. Now I'll make some coffee and you can tell me what kind of trouble you got into."

"Anyone that knows you at all would know that's bullshit."

"Corporate level people don't associate with us peons," I said. "Everything was decided at a corporate level. I'm guessin' they were gettin' some heat after losin' three whole crews and havin' to pay the fees to download into new clones. They needed a fall guy, and I was the one that came back every time."

"Three times? You were the only one to come back three times?"

"Yeah." I leaned back in the chair and took a sip of the coffee. "Reckon I'm pretty good at killin' folks."

He let out a long sigh.

"What?"

"Reckon it runs in your blood, kid. Your dad was hell on wheels in a fight too."

"He never talked about it," I said.

"Do you talk about it if it's not dragged out of you?"

"Not so much."

"I didn't think so. So now I'm draggin'. Tell me all of it."

"I don't really want to talk about it," I said.

"You got to talk to someone, kid."

"It's all more of the same, Pops."

He took a sip from his coffee mug. "It's probably not, but I'll let you slide for now. Any ideas what you're gonna do? Do you plan to stay here or are you still too messed up over that girl?"

"Not sure what I'll do, now. Found out a few things that change my situation with Ginger, though. Gonna have to go see her before I make any decisions."

"You sure that's a good idea, kid?"

"Probably not, but I have to see her."

"You know about the shakes?" he asked.

"I just found out."

"That explains a whole lot about what went down."

"You know? Did everybody know but me?"

"Small community, kid. She hid it well, but everything comes out in time." He set his empty coffee mug on the side table. "It don't take a genius to see what happened there."

"I wouldn't have left, Pop."

"I figured. It was too late once I found out. You were gone and I never had any way to contact you. I'm a little pissed about that. You could have given me a number or somethin' to call. Just up and disappeared."

"Didn't want to be contacted, Pop. I should've sent word once I got over that. Didn't want to admit I was the asshole."

"Well you're here now." He grinned. "Asshole."

Chapter 9

The power plant hummed as we accelerated down Hickory Valley Road. My helmet had a direct connection to the sensors and my HUD showed a topographical representation of the surrounding area. The mini drones flew overhead, resembling nothing more than birds flying over. I liked the triple drone pattern for the better coverage.

"Still lookin' clear?" Pops asked.

"Not used to havin' a second?"

"Force of habit. I'm usually running this on my own. I flashed the HUD every thirty seconds to keep track."

"You just drive, Pops. I'll holler if I get a hit."

"Fine."

"When did you start deliverin' to the Flatfords?"

"Figured it was easier to deal with them than Maynardville. As long as we have somethin' they like, we're good with Rob."

Flatfords had been in Hickory Valley for ages. Rob was the clan head, being a direct descendant of old Bobby Flatford who had established the clan after the Second Civil War, about six years before the Blight. Bobby and his brother had been there for years but when the war was done, they had begun to fortify. When a lot of the area was sinking into chaos, they stepped in and brought order. Iron fisted order, but order, nonetheless.

"If I knew you were dealin' with them, I could have just made a leisurely stroll through here on my way home."

"And whose fault is that?"

I grunted.

"I'm lookin' at you, asshole."

"Well look at the road. You're drivin'."

He chuckled.

"We got a couple of vehicles incoming on Hurricane Holler."

I armed the rockets and spun up the minigun.

"Give 'em a minute to recognize. You ain't got no faith in the peacableness of mankind?"

Both incoming vehicles halted and did three-point turns.

"I don't think that's a word, Pop. Force of habit. Incoming usually means the bullets are about to fly. Reckon your reputation precedes you," I said.

"It does. I haven't had to fight Charlene but once on this run. They found out right quick it wasn't profitable. Then I set up the deliveries to Rob and they had a bigger reason to leave me be."

"I still find it funny you named the car after Grandma's sister instead of her."

"Still not gonna talk about that."

"Come on, Pops. We all know you had a thing for her."

"Not gonna talk about it."

I laughed.

"So there's a pretty big group ahead at Highway 61. What about their peacableness?"

"That's Rob. He ain't much on peacableness, but he sure likes my shine, so I reckon there won't be any violenceness."

"Really?"

"What?" He chuckled.

"Never mind. Just let me know if we need any of that violenceness."

I could see his grin beneath the visor of his helmet. I had missed him over the last six years. I needed to get away from there, but I should have stayed in touch.

We rolled to a stop alongside an old armored truck that had been converted into a mobile battle wagon.

"Sure as hell wouldn't want to meet that if he was interested in violenceness," I said.

"Yep." He powered down. "We ain't in hostile territory here, Jake. Relax."

I nodded and took my hand away from the control yoke for the mini gun.

The gun port closed, and Rob Flatford stepped out of the passenger side of the armored truck.

Pops got out of the car, and I followed suit.

"Thought you were still pissed about that last card game, Larry."

Rob Flatford didn't look like he would be all that he was rumored to be. He was in his forties with salt and pepper grey in his hair. He wasn't large but not really small either. Average was the word I would use to describe him. At least until you looked in his eyes. I could see a lot of death in those eyes. I knew that look because it was the same look I saw when I looked into a mirror.

"Nah, this is my grandson, Jake. Just got home from workin' road crews in Knoxville so he's a little high strung."

"Road crews?" Rob looked closer.

I chuckled. "Everyone does that. I'm still original."

"That's not the way it usually goes with a road crew."

"True enough."

"Jake, huh?"

"Yup."

"I may have heard some rumors about a fella named Jake who worked the road crew guards. You wouldn't be that Jake, would you?"

"Depends on the rumors." My eye twitched.

"I used to trade some, well… product we grow around here with a bunch out around Crossville."

My eye twitched again.

"Before you get all riled up, I didn't have much use for that bunch. But they had control of a route I needed to use when bypassing certain authorities in Knoxville. I had some people disappear over there only to show back up about five years ago. They were in pretty rough shape, but they told some stories about one particular night a few days after this bunch hit a road crew."

I let out a long breath.

"Was a fella that got loose amongst this bunch of savages. He'd been tortured for days, and I reckon he was right pissed about it. Way Angie described it, the fella went through that bunch like some sort of demon. Rumor was that he killed everyone, but Angie said he freed her and a few other people before he disappeared into the night."

"You know how rumors are," Pop said. "People make up all sorts of things."

"You're probably right, Larry," Rob said. "Were I to meet this fella, I would like to thank him. Angie is my wife now and that never would have happened without this demon from the road crews."

He stepped forward and held out his hand. "It's good to meet you, Jake."

I shook his hand, and he gave an extra squeeze at the end. He nodded as he stared into my eyes.

Stepping back, he said, "Alright, boys. Let's get this load moved over to the truck."

Chapter 10

I stood outside leaning on Charlene while Pop finished his deal with Rob.

"Shame we don't have time for another game this time," Rob said as they stepped down from the back of the truck. "I'd love to whip your ass again, Larry."

"Next time, I'll be doin' the whippin', youngster. You know age and treachery beats youth and vigor."

"I'm beginning to agree, old timer. I can't do what I used to." They stopped at the front of the armored truck. "I owe your boy, there, more than you can ever know, Turner. My home is yours. You and yours are welcome anytime to sup at my table. If help is ever needed, it is freely given."

He was looking straight at me as he said it, and I gave a small nod, so he knew I understood.

I never asked who the others being held were. It didn't matter. They were being held by rapists and killers. Frankly, I wasn't in any shape to do more than open their cage before I staggered into the night. If not for another stranger, there would have been a brand new me out there with no memory of what happened that night. Sometimes, I didn't know whether to thank the man or curse him. I would have loved to forget those days of hell and what I did after.

The road crews were no place for anyone raised like I was. Many of the same ones who knew me before would have vilified a clone with my memories. Sometimes religion can be a bitch. I didn't think Pop would have treated the clone differently, but who knows until it's staring you in the face?

He was quiet for a bit after we got back into Charlene and donned our helmets. He waved at the Flatfords as we turned the car and drove back up Hickory Valley toward home.

"I'm guessin' that's what you didn't want to talk about."

"Maybe."

"Things just have a way of comin' out, kid. You keep that stuff bottled up inside and there ain't no tellin' what sort of damage it does to you."

"TTA sent me to a shrink after that."

"Did it help?"

"Not that I could tell. Their shrinks weren't much anyway. They spent the majority of their time talkin' to clones while they adjusted to the reality they had died. They didn't see this kind of shit regularly."

"And the other two times?"

"Nothin' like that one. They didn't even bother with the shrink after the second one. Third, they just fired me."

"Sure wish you'd just stayed home."

"Sometimes, I do too."

"Everything clear?"

"I thought we already covered that," I said. "I'll holler if there's an issue. Just drive."

"Fine."

"Need to swing by Jackie's and drop off that last case, too," I said.

"Now there's a fine young woman that would really suit you, kid."

"Shit Pop, she ain't into my type."

"What? She don't like assholes?"

"She doesn't like men, Pop."

"Damn."

"I agree," I said. "Knowin' my luck, her and Ginger will get together and I'll have to watch both women that I care for run off together."

"Sounds about right."

"Geez, you could argue a little."

"Why bother?" he shrugged. "She's a lot prettier than you. Odds are in her favor."

"Now who's bein' the asshole?"

He grinned.

We were quiet for a bit, and I kept my eyes on the sensors and my hands on the weapon controls. I kept my attention on our surroundings so I wouldn't have to think of other stuff.

Of course Pop couldn't keep his trap shut and let that happen.

"What are you gonna do about Ginger now that you know?"

"Can't just leave things be, can you?"

"You ever known me to leave things be?"

I sighed. "Can't rightly say I have."

"Then why would you expect me to now?"

"Not sure what to do, Pops. If my name was clear, I'd see if she wanted to go join the road crew so she could get a Gold Cross upload. Looks like that ship has sailed. Buying one of those packages would assure she could keep going. Frankly, I don't even know if she would do it. You know what folks around here think of that."

"There're other ways to go about it, too, kid."

"I'd have to do some seriously shady shit to make that kind of money."

"I'm not talkin' bout workin' for the Hillbilly Mafia," he said.

"What then?"

"You know who my wife was before we married and bought this place."

"She was a Graven, wasn't she?"

"Yeah."

"Like the ones in Kentucky?"

"Exactly like the ones in Kentucky."

"She was one of the Gravens in Bowling Green?"

"Yep."

"You mean autoduelling, then? Go die for the cameras?"

"That's what I'm talking about."

"It takes money to buy into that," I said. "And you have to win enough to be able to get Gold Cross. Then you have to keep winnin' enough keep it."

"What if I told you all you have to do is win one amateur night in Knoxville? The prize is a Platinum package at Gold Cross and entry into this big cross-country race they're settin' up. I'm talkin' platinum. Lifetime package."

"You already been thinkin' of this?"

"It's been one of those old man pipe dreams. I couldn't make it with Charlene. She's tough as nails out here in the sticks but there's a lot of youngsters with a lot of cash rollin' in Amateur Night. Not sure if I could do it."

"I don't have a car, Pop."

"I think you could figure something out."

I could see something playing out in my head. She could drive anything with wheels, and it might save her, if she was willing to be saved that way. We had spent those years talking about a lot of things, but we both shied away from religion. She might refuse from the start.

But what if she didn't? What if we could do this thing? Was there a chance that we could still…?

Chapter 11

"What are the chances I could get you to build me a battle wagon if it turns out I need it?"

The phone was silent for a moment before Jackie answered, "What the hell do you need a battle wagon for?"

"Pop has an in with the folks who run autoduelling in the area."

"And why are you even interested in that?"

"There's a thing comin' up. Winning team gets a Gold Cross Platinum plan."

"Gold Cross, huh?"

"To win, I need a damn good car, a damn good greaser, and a damn good driver."

"I see. I don't have to look too deep to figure out the why. But the how is still a big question."

"The severance pay from TTA is the how."

"Isn't that everything you have?"

"I've been broke before," I said. "This is important enough to do."

"What's she think about it?"

"Don't know yet. Needed to see if it's feasible."

She was quiet for a moment. "I can build you one hell of a wagon, but the weaponry?"

"I'll get the weapons."

"Told you ... hero complex."

"I ain't no hero. If I'd stuck around a little while longer ..."

"That's not on you, Jake. She did that."

"We did that," I said. "She did her part, but I did too. I left without even finding out why. Maybe I can make up for my part by giving her a way out. Maybe she can make up for hers by taking it."

"You know this is insane, right?" she asked. "I can build your wagon. Go see if her stubborn ass will agree to it."

"Insane? No more than runnin' off and joinin' the road crews. I'll be at the races tonight. I can see what she says."

"You have a point. Good luck, hero."

I grunted. "Ain't no hero."

Race night at the Tazewell Speedway was one of the biggest nights of the month. It was straight up old fashioned racing. They liked the classics in Tazewell. It was all about speed and intestinal fortitude. There were no weapons unless you considered a ton of race car running at two hundred miles per hour a weapon.

Drivers were there to win but not trying to kill one another. There had been some incidents in the past when drivers tried to crash the others, but they'd been dealt with pretty harshly. It was a contest of skill, not savagery.

Tickets could be bought or bartered at the entry.

"Jake frackin' Turner! Is that you?"

"Kelly." I stepped up to the ticket kiosk. "How you doin'?"

"I'm good, Jake. Just surprised to see you. I thought you were dead."

"Not yet."

"Is that a jar of Larry's shine?" Kelly Arnold asked. "You know that's good for a ticket and then some."

"Figured it would do."

"Figured?" Kelly laughed. Then he shook his head and looked closely at me. "Word was you got killed."

"Checkin' to see if I'm a clone?"

He straightened up.

"No worries, Kelly. I'm not."

"Sometimes you just gotta be careful, Jake. You know what the boss thinks of clones."

"He'll have issues with them until he gets close to the end. Reckon that'll change, then."

Kelly chuckled. "Probably right. That jar there'll get you a ticket and a food and drink voucher if that's what you brought it for."

"Yup."

He handed me a ticket stub and two plastic chits as I set the jar on the counter. He leaned closer. "If you're here to see Ginger, be careful. Tommy's set his eyes on her."

"She agreed to that?"

"You know Tommy Payne. Agreed or not, she's off limits to anyone else. But she hasn't made a fuss, so I expect it's mutual."

"I sure didn't miss this part of livin' up here. And you also know me. Tommy Payne can kiss my ass."

He scratched his head and grinned. "Yep, Jake's back. Things might get lively round here."

"He doesn't start anything, there won't be anything."

"You're still crazy as hell, ain't you?"

I grinned.

Kelly shook his head. "Enjoy the race, Jake."

I pocketed the chits and wandered around the stands a bit before settling in the top row of the stadium seating right in the corner. I sat and rested my right hand just an inch from my hand cannon.

"Not in hostile territory," I muttered to myself.

The cars were already lined up at the starting line. There would be a pre-selected amount of laps around the large oval track with the ends banked up so the drivers wouldn't need to slow as much for them. The cars were rigorously inspected and as close to equal as they could be. The race would be decided by skill. Skill and guts.

Pop said Ginger was driving one of Douglas Payne's cars. Payne usually had several racers working for him so one of his cars was almost always in the races held at Tazewell Speedway. She was driving the second car in the lineup, and I could see her just well enough to see the splash of red where her hair hung out of the bottom of her helmet.

I let out a long breath as memories of her ran through my mind and a lot of the pain I'd felt came back to the surface. All I had felt before I left was pain and betrayal. I thought I had put all of that behind me, but it still came up gnawing at the surface of my thoughts. The old bitterness was still there in the back of my mind.

"This whole plan is just a fool's errand," I muttered. "What was I thinkin'?"

My hand slid a little closer to the hand cannon on my hip as I recognized the fellows that moved in my direction. Tommy Payne had climbed the stadium and walked out the top row in my direction as several others walked out the rows below me in case I chose to run.

Tommy was about six feet tall, blonde, blue-eyed, and handsome. His clothes were colorful, and I was sure I'd seen their like on the vids. Maybe one of the autoduel teams. He was a quarterback when we were in school.

Popularity was a big thing then and his family's stature in Tazewell was an even bigger thing after we all graduated.

He was surprised when I didn't try to run, and I wasn't sure why that was. I'd never been one to run from trouble. I guessed he had just gotten used to the fear everyone else afforded him.

"Tommy," I said and motioned toward the seat beside me. "Have a seat."

"I think you need to leave, Turner. You're not welcome here."

"Now, Tommy, I already bought my ticket and everything."

"That doesn't change anything, Turner."

I was on my feet in an instant and the suddenness of it gave him a start. Then I could see the flush of rage he felt as he realized I had seen it. I didn't say a word, but my hand hung very close to the hand cannon.

He saw the stance and smirked. As his eyes raised to mine, the smirk dropped from his features, and he was visibly taken aback. He saw something there and he didn't like it one bit.

"She doesn't want anything to do with you, Jake."

"That may be true, Tommy." My gaze never faltered. "She made that pretty clear years ago. But I'll speak to her, nevertheless. Now the next move is up to you. You can start somethin' that gets real ugly or you can have a seat and watch the race with me. We'll crack open a jar of Pop's shine and watch like old times."

He slowly nodded his head and waved off the two thugs who'd been set to block me in. Letting out a long breath, he sat in the seat I had motioned toward and looked over at me.

"So, where you been for the last six years, Jake?"

I sat back in my seat and pulled a pint jar from the pack I had carried with me.

Chapter 12

"How many laps they doin' now?" I asked.

"It's a mile track and they're runnin' a twenty-mile race," Tommy said.

"Still get hairy out there at the first turn?"

"Every time."

"Used to be the place where the race was always decided."

The flag dropped and the cars surged forward.

"It still is. It takes some skill to take it at speed and some drivers have to slow more than others," he said. "Ginger and Reese are the main contenders tonight."

"Andy Reese?"

"Yeah, he started racin' a couple years back. He's a natural like Ginger."

"She always could drive anything with wheels."

"Still can," he said. He turned and looked at me. "Even with the shakes."

"I recently learned about that," I said.

"I wondered."

"What?"

"Why the boy scout would just run off and leave her to deal with it alone. I had a sneaky suspicion you didn't know about it."

I was quiet as I watched the cars round the first turn. Two cars gained almost a whole car length in that small amount of time.

"I see what you mean, Reese took that corner as fast as she did."

"He's a hell of a racer."

"His family build the car?" I asked.

"You know they did."

"Ginger drivin' yours?"

"She's drivin' one of my dad's cars."

"Figured as much." I turned to him. "I'm gonna put my cards on the table here, Tommy. Do you love her?"

"Well that's kind of a loaded question."

"Let me put it this way. I've discovered some things while workin' the road crews. There's a way she can live past this thing she has. I have a plan. Certain connections can get us entered into a special autoduel event. We win the event, we get entered into this new thing they are cookin' up called the Dead Man's Run. Entry comes with a Gold Cross Platinum package. You see where I'm goin' with this. My question to you is this: can you provide an alternative?"

"Damn, Jake, you did just find out, didn't you?"

"That's what I said."

"My family could afford Gold Cross, but you know how it is around here. We'd have to run off and start new somewhere else."

"That's why I asked the first question, and, yes, it's a loaded question. Do you love her enough to do that?"

"I don't know if I could."

"See, Tommy, I know what I'll give and it's everything I got."

"I can't stand in the way of that, Jake. I knew you were a boy scout but six years ago you wouldn't have done somethin' like this. You've changed. What happened to you out there? You said the road crews? Are you a clone?"

"Still the original, Tommy. But I saw a lot of folks go through it and they were the same people they were before. I never was overly religious, but it worried me still."

"Damn it, Jake."

"I know, right? It's a lot to process but I have to make her the offer." I handed him the jar of authentic corn whiskey, a rarity since most corn was destroyed years ago. "Let's drink a few and watch the race."

Fifteen laps in; Ginger and Andy were still right there together. Andy had been in the lead car and Ginger was right behind him when they started. She was running beside him by this lap.

"She'll take him on the turn this time," Tommy said. "He'll flinch."

"She's less than a foot from him."

"She'll get closer on the turn."

He was right. As they entered the turn, she was only a couple of inches from the side of Andy's car. Halfway through, he pulled away from her and lost ground as she took the inside of the turn.

The crowd cheered.

"She's got more nerve than any other driver out there," I said.

"But autoduelling?" he shook his head. "People are dying out there in the arenas."

"I know. I never had much use for it but what else can I do? What can I do that pays enough to get one of those packages? She's the best damn driver I've ever seen."

"So what's that make you, Jake? You gonna be a gunner?"

"I reckon."

"Everyone in that arena will want to kill you."

"Think so?"

"A Gold Cross Platinum? You're damn right."

"Reckon I'm used to that," I muttered.

"They say the road crews are bad, Jake, are they right?"

"They're as bad as it gets, Tommy. Can't stay in one spot too long or they have time to gather a bunch of assholes to come after you. Road crews are always still for days at a time."

"I've heard some of the rumors. They say a whole crew was wiped out about a month ago. One guy came back."

"You know how rumors are, Tommy," I said. "You can't set much store in 'em."

We were both quiet for a while as we watched Andy hover right on Ginger's bumper, but he never made up the distance he lost when she took the lead. The final lap finished with her a single car length ahead of him.

"What say we go ask her what she thinks of it?" he asked.

I followed him down the stands and out to the track where she climbed out of the driver side of the car. She was just as beautiful as I remembered, five feet six with the body of a runner. She removed the helmet and red hair blew in the wind. Turning toward our approach, the smile on her face froze. Shock turned to joy for a moment, and I thought there might just be a chance. Then it transformed into something colder.

"Maybe I should talk to her first," Tommy said.

"I reckon so."

Chapter 13

"So you're plan is for me to die?" she asked with a snarl.

"That's not what I'm sayin', and you know it." My voice was abrupt, and she was a little taken aback. "I'm sharing what I've learned and offering what I can do to help you."

"I don't need your pity."

I nodded and walked away.

"That was about as stupid a thing I've ever seen you do, girl," Tommy said as I walked away. "Did you see his eyes? There's no pity left in that man."

"What?"

I walked out of hearing range and moved into the crowd. I was seething inside but I never let it show.

Her nerve was one of the greatest things about her but also the most infuriating. She sent me away six years ago with no explanation. I went down a path of self-destruction, taking the most dangerous job I could find. I was tortured nearly to death, and it turned me into a killer.

Six years later and all I could see in her was rage. But there was that moment … I'd spent six years wondering what I did to drive her away from what we were creating and punishing myself for that unknown. Knowing why she did it didn't change anything about what I'd done and what I'd become.

Did I still love her? Maybe. No one can upset a person more than someone he cares about.

The Spider hummed to life as I approached and hit the fob. It was a good bike, but I would hate to be using one of them for any sort of fight inside of one of the arenas. I wasn't fond of watching the duels, but I wasn't oblivious. They were the biggest thing in the country. Deathball had been at the top for some time, but it faded into the background when the autoduels became a thing. I felt like it might be fading just as Deathball did.

What little I had caught on the vids about the Dead Man's Run might be enough to bring it back to life. They were keeping most of the details close to their vests but the gist of it was a long range run across the country. The whole year ahead of us was dedicated to qualifying for the run. It wasn't all based in Knoxville either. There were others beginning in Atlanta, Virginia Beach, and several other parts of the country.

Pops said the rumor was that Knoxville was running a special series of Amateur Nights where teams would build their cars for the event and last man standing made it into the roster for the Dead Man's Run. Every month over the next year they would have events until there were twelve teams to participate in the Run.

There were limits to what you could build for one of the matches – it had to be an AADA approved build with a limit on what you could arm it with. I had enough in that severance package to build a car. But it was pointless to think about it if she wouldn't accept the help offered.

I couldn't just sit here in Tazewell and watch her degenerate either. Chattanooga was my best bet to continue with a road crew. There was nothing out there aside from blood sports that paid as well as that. Nothing legal anyway. Maybe in ten years I could put together enough to buy her one of…

"Shit."

I guess I still did love her.

"Can't save someone who doesn't want to be saved," I muttered as I exited the speedway and headed toward Morristown.

The other end of Lone Mountain Road was a couple of miles in that direction. Thumbing the accelerator, I shot down Highway 25 faster than I should have. I passed a Bulldog driving the other way and he flashed his blue lights as he passed. I dropped the speed back down and he continued on his way.

Speed limits were pretty fluid on the roads, but they would pull you for recklessness. I couldn't argue with that. I was moving faster than was really safe. I had been letting my rage get the best of me.

I understood what she did six years ago. I was having a hard time understanding her reaction today. Mostly, I saw anger. But there was that moment…

I focused on my sensors to keep me distracted the rest of the way to Pop's. I thumbed the fob and the gate opened. Parking the Spider, I walked inside and up the stairs without a word.

Pop was sitting in his chair reading one of his books.

"Looks like that went well," I heard him say just before I closed the door to the bedroom.

I was sitting on the bed close to an hour later when the buzzer for the gate went off. I heard Pop moving downstairs. Standing, I watched out the window as a gray pick-up pulled through the opened gate.

"Shit," I muttered.

I sat back down on the bed as I heard Pop open the door and took the quart jar from the bedside table.

"Thank you, Mister Turner," she said as he let her inside.

I took a deep drink of the fiery liquid in the jar.

She stepped into the room and closed the door behind her.

"You know I can't stand it when you just walk off," she said. "Last time you didn't come back."

"You were pretty clear about what you wanted, then."

"And you disappeared for six years?" Her green eyes narrowed.

"What did you expect, Gin? You didn't give me any explanation why I wasn't good enough, so I left."

She shook her head. "You were always good enough. I was the one that was broken. Where the hell have you been?"

"I been workin' in Knoxville."

"And you couldn't let anyone know where you were?"

"I didn't want anyone to know."

She was quiet for a moment. "So you think uploading me into a computer is the solution to this?" She held a shaky right hand up.

"It's a solution, Gin. Not sayin' it's the best one."

"Tommy says you were workin' for the road crews." She stepped closer. "Are you a clone, Jake?"

"I'm not." I rolled back my sleeve to show her the scar on the back of my left shoulder. "Remember where I got that?"

She chuckled. "Tire tool stabbed you while we were in the back of my truck."

"Yeah, clones don't come with the scars."

"I thought all the road crews were clones."

"The majority of them are," I said rolling my sleeve back down. "I have several friends that came back just like they were before, so I have my doubts about what we were taught."

I was pretty sure that was why the road crews were so dangerous. A lot of people think clones are soulless so they can do whatever they please to them.

"How does it work?"

"I don't rightly know the specifics. Took a month or so until the crews came back to the shop after."

"What do we have to do?"

"Win one of the autodueling runs on Amateur Night over the next year. The winners are entered into Dead Man's Run. The sponsor has guaranteed a platinum plan for all of the sponsored."

"And what is this Dead Man's Run?"

"They're about to start pushin' it on the networks. Pop said it's a long distance run from city to city across the country. Details are just coming to the autoduel community where Pop has connections."

"What makes you think we could win a race?"

"I never saw anyone who could drive better than you, Gin."

"There's more to it than driving."

"You worry about the drivin', Gin. I'll take care of the rest." Something familiar and cold moved inside of me.

She stared into my eyes and gasped. "What's happened to you, Jake?"

I pushed the killer back under the surface. "Life, I reckon."

Life and death. A lot of death.

"She looks a little shook up," Pop said as Ginger got into her truck and backed out of the drive.

"She should be. What we're lookin' at is a fight to the death with a bunch of others who want the same thing we do. She's never had to do that."

"You'll keep her safe?"

"Safe as I can, Pop." I leaned on the porch rail and watched her drive out the gate. "Go on and call 'em. We'll get ready. I need to know what we need to pull together."

"I'll know as soon as they call. They may do a build your own or they may supply the cars. I've seen both scenarios. Charlie will know."

I chuckled.

"Oh shut up. Your grandma's been gone a long time."

"You never named a car after her."

He shrugged. "I'll call Charlie tonight."

"Thanks Pop."

"Don't thank me till you see what this thing is all about. They're offering a platinum plan, it has to be something pretty tough. You may want to cuss me instead."

Chapter 14

"They have two 'build your own' matches this year and the rest are supplied by the sponsors. There's a problem with it though."

"What is it, Pop?"

"The whole thing in Knoxville is sponsored by Tennessee Titan Authority."

"Shit." I sat in the chair across the table. "Where does that leave us?"

"I told Charlie about your problem with TTA, and she said we can use it. It won't be pleasant."

"How?"

"They'll use it as a selling point for getting you in the arena. There's no way it doesn't go on the big screens. This doesn't work, it'll burn you in every city after this. She's worth all this?"

"Would you have done it for Gran?"

"Yeah." He took a sip of coffee. "But Lizzie never sent me packing when shit got real. I didn't go out and try to get killed because of her."

"And turned myself into a killer."

"You did what you did to survive, kid," he said. "You were a soldier in a war. Soldiers have been doing that for hundreds of years. We don't fight wars anymore, officially. But what's happening to the road crews is as close to a war as anything we ever fought as a nation in the old days."

"I'll do what I have to, Pop. She was everything to me, once."

"Once?"

"I'm not him anymore, Pop. I'm something else now but I'll try my best to give her a future."

"There's more of him left than you think, kid." He stood up and took the empty coffee cup back to the pot. "You'll see."

I grunted as I drained the last of the coffee in my cup.

"Got a way with words, don't you?" he asked.

"Heh."

"Well, quit grunting at me and go feed the damn cow. I'll be along shortly to milk her."

"I can do it."

"You never could milk worth a damn. That's why she kicked the bucket over more times than not. She's even touchier now. Nothin' gentle about you, kid. I don't reckon that's any different now."

I laughed and set my cup in the sink.

The air was crisp as I stepped outside and there was a touch of frost on the grass. I stopped and just listened for a couple of minutes. It was quiet and peaceful. Then the rooster started crowing.

I chuckled. So much for quiet.

Was I doing the right thing, dragging Ginger into that meat grinder they called the autoduel circuit? I wasn't sure what we were getting into, but I knew it would be violent. I could do violence, but I wasn't sure about her. She had an iron will, but was it enough for what we would have to do? It would have to be.

"Hey Millie," I said as I stepped into the barn where the Jersey cow had her head over the gate to her stall. "You ready for some grub?"

I dragged a hay bale off of the pile and pulled my knife from my hip to cut the strings. I tossed half of it into the hay bin as I heard a vehicle crunching through the gravel of the drive. I looked out the door to see Ginger's truck.

I started to step out, but the gate opened again, and another vehicle entered. Jackie drove an old truck from the days before weaponized vehicles. It was running on old style tires and lifted. I was pretty sure it was her Grandpa's old truck. It used to be called a Power Wagon back before the major auto companies went under. How she kept it running, I had no idea.

Ginger got out of her truck and watched Jackie park. Jackie jumped out of the Power Wagon and walked toward Ginger shaking her finger.

"What the frack were you thinkin', Red?"

"What?"

"What do you think?" she asked. "You didn't tell him?"

"You see what happened when he found out."

"Yeah, I do. He'll go out there and …"

"What? What can I do to stop him? You know how he is when he gets the bit in his teeth."

"You should have told him."

"You don't think I know that, Jack? When I realized it, he was gone."

"How is not telling him your first choice, dumbass? Do you even know what he did after that?"

"He said he worked in Knoxville for the road crews."

"Is that all he said? He's as big a dumbass as you are."

"What happened?"

"That's something you should ask him."

"It's that bad?"

"Worse."

"I can only say I'm sorry so many times, Jack."

"Have you? Have you actually told him you're sorry? Have you told me you're sorry for making me angry with my friend for years because he left you in the lurch? You could have at least told me so I wouldn't hate him all that time."

"I am sorry, Jack. When he disappeared, it was so much easier to not be the asshole. I made a mistake. I wish I could change the past, but I can't."

"If there's a single good thing that it did, it put him where he could see that clones aren't evil or soulless. Maybe there's a chance you can survive this thing."

"I'm going with him because I'm not a victim, Jack. He's not my white knight come to save me. There's not another driver in this state that can do it better. He's always been a fighter, but driving is where it counts."

"You really need to talk to him about what he's been doing for the last five years, girl."

Chapter 15

"And the Twin Terrors have taken the victory! Amateur Night is getting hot tonight! No less than three burning wrecks on the arena floor and the Twins join the roster for the event of the decade!"

"Have you seen the new sponsorship for Amateur Night from Graven Industries, Gavin?" the pretty news anchor asked her co-anchor.

"I haven't seen the details yet, but it's rumored they have a real peach, Ellen. What do you know? I'm sure our viewers are on the edge of their seats."

"A driver from the local area who has dominated the Tazewell Speedway for the last five years, Ginger Yates. But the real head turner is her gunner. It took a little digging but he's the one they're calling the Butcher of the I75 Corridor."

"Oh my, Ellen! The I-75 Butcher was featured in the news a few months ago. Sole survivor from a raider attack on one of the road crews."

"One and the same, Gavin. But this wasn't the first time he was the sole survivor, either. This was no less than his third time."

"Three times? That's remarkable! The man has more kills than many veteran gunners. This should be an interesting addition to next month's competition. How will the Butchers stack up against the other competitors? Tune in next month and we'll all find out together!"

I turned off the TV.

Ginger was staring at me with wide eyes.

"They said it was going to come out pretty quickly once we were signed up," I said.

"I saw the news when they covered it. How did you not say that was you?"

I stared at her.

She sighed.

"What happened to you, Jake? Jackie won't tell me, and Pop just points me to you."

I pointed at the TV. "Reckon they just said it."

"They lie as much as they tell the truth," she said.

"They told the truth this time. Not too happy about the name, though."

"Who decided what we were called?"

"Our sponsors. They wanted to take advantage of that I-75 thing."

"I thought they were your family."

"They are. But they know the world we're goin' into. Charlie says ratings are everything in this game and we'll need to play it to the hilt if we plan to get anywhere. Sucks that the platinum package is a sign-on for the Dead Man's Run instead of a victory prize for the match."

"I guess Jackie is relieved she doesn't have to build us a vehicle since we didn't manage to get one of those two 'build your own' nights."

"She was a little disappointed to be honest." I stepped into the kitchen to refill my coffee cup. "She doesn't trust anyone else's work."

"Probably right."

I sat down at the table as the gate buzzer went off.

"Damn thing goes off every ten minutes," Pop muttered as he walked in from the living room. "Went off once a month when you were gone."

"It's probably Tommy," she said. "He said he'd come by this evening. Not sure what he's up to though. He's been acting weird."

I had my suspicions about what was up with Tommy. He had been acting squirrely from the moment I had brought up the clones. He was raised just like we had been.

She looked out the window to see Tommy's car pulling up out front. She stepped out the door to meet him. I didn't really like Tommy Payne, but I'm fairly sure I wouldn't like anyone she chose to see. Jackie was even surprised when she found out Ginger had been seeing him.

She met him as he got out of the car, and I could see some words exchange. I couldn't hear them, but I could see her face and the flash of anger at what he was saying.

"Reckon he's breakin' it off," Pop said as he sat down at the table. "The clone thing is too much for a lot of folks."

"Reckon so."

She turned away and, instead of coming back inside, got in her truck. She spun up some gravel as she drove back down the drive and out the gate.

Tommy just stood there.

I reached into the fridge, pulled out a half empty quart, and walked outside. Walking over to Tommy, I opened the lid, and handed him the jar.

"Why do I feel like the bad guy here?"

"Hard to wrap your mind around the whole thing, Tommy," I said. "Took me several years and a few friends who went through it before I could accept it. I don't believe the same things now that I used to. I don't know what to believe at this point."

"Didn't you go to the road crews the same year you left?"

"It wasn't for the Gold Cross, man."

He sighed as he realized what I was saying. "You were there to die."

"Found out I wasn't any good at it. Dying."

"I guess so. The news has been going wild over your being in the next match. They've been talking about the I-75 Butcher a lot. You really kill that whole lot?"

I took a swig from the jar. "I saw my whole squad get taken out by a rocket and these guys were standing around the burning wreckage joking about it. So, yeah, I killed 'em."

"Some networks are claiming rumors that you were working with the raiders." He turned to look at me. "Reckon that's bullshit, though. I can't see that at all."

"They'll say all sorts of things. The Gravens told me to expect that and a lot more as this starts getting' ramped up over the next month."

"I expect so. You ready for all of it to be out there?"

"Not really, but what choice do I have?"

"You could be like everyone else, Jake," he said. "You could live your life and let go of the past."

"Too late for that, Tommy."

"Never too late for it, Jake."

"Can't take back the things I've done. Best to use 'em for someone who needs 'em."

He took a long drink from the jar and passed it back to me. "Frackin' boy scout."

Chapter 16

"**T**his month's matchup is certainly going to be interesting, folks. I've just learned that the second sponsored entry into Amateur Night are the Rabble Rousers! This team is sponsored by a professional driving team, the notorious Vixens! As you well know, the Vixens have been known to use tactics that are downright dirty to win in the arena. Can we expect any less from a team under their sponsorship?

"Third are the Fountain City Foundation's own team, The Orange Crush! Kaleb Young has been driving for the Crush in quite a few local events, but this is his first time getting into Amateur Night. His gunner is none other than his quick shooting wife, Jasmine, who has been the reigning gunnery champion in Knoxville for the last three years!

"How will the Blacktop Butchers stand with these two? We'll just have to see!" Gavin Grey's voice lowered conspiratorially. "Speaking of butchers, I've heard some disturbing rumors about the events around the I-75 Butcher's career. I heard from some of the road crew themselves as they talk about the reason Turner was let go at the TTA. It seems some of them are convinced he was working with the very raiders that attacked their crews. What kind of man is he? And what can we expect from him in the arena? I guess we'll see at the end of the month! Be sure to tune in to..."

I turned the radio off.

"Already sick of hearing about it?" Pop asked.

"Just watching any future of getting work later go down the tubes," I said as I grabbed another case of liquor and loaded it on the pallet. "If I get through this, all I'll be able to do is haul shine."

"It's not a bad gig, kid."

"Odds are it would be a clone of me. What then?"

"You'll be my grandson."

I turned and stared at him. "Thanks Pop."

"My suggestion would be not to get yourself killed out there."

"That's the ideal solution," I said. "But the more I look at what they're settin' up, the less I feel like it's the most likely solution. They want blood for the masses, Pop. Since they started talkin' about the Run, the ratings have been steadily climbin'."

"I know, kid. That's the autoduelling world. It's all about ratings." He added another case to the pallet. "Son, you're gonna have to play to the crowds. Look at this."

He pulled a pamphlet from his pocket and handed it to me. It was an early sign-up ad for a package that would let the buyer 'ride' in the car with one of the teams during the race. Access to the cameras inside the vehicle as well as voice access at certain times.

"That's just beautiful," I said in disgust.

"It's a new thing they've started doing in some of the events. They'll probably have some of them in the car at Amateur Night."

"Just gets better and better. They want a close-up when we die."

"Just something to remember when you get out there. You having second thoughts yet?"

"I'm on fifth or sixth by now and you're not helpin'. It's like every day you bring some other little kernel of shit to show me."

He stood still for a minute. "Thing is, kid, this whole thing was my idea. It's my job to make sure you're as prepared as I can make you."

"I know, Pop. I'm just bitchin' to keep my mind off of some of it. I'm just afraid I'll take her into that arena and get her killed."

"And I'm afraid I'll have sent my grandson off to die. Ain't we a pair?"

"A pair of fools, I reckon."

"Yup." He looked at the pallet of whiskey. "I'll get the lift and we'll load up Charlene. This is goin' to Morristown and those Bean Station boys might be hankerin' for a scrap."

"I'll get the ammo bins filled up. You got some rockets for the magazine?"

"Just a couple."

"Then I'll put one reload on each side."

"Got plenty of ammo for the miniguns."

"That's what I like to hear."

"I don't think they'll give us any trouble but best to be prepared. They may still be bent out of shape about the guys at Arby Keck's place."

"Jackie told me about that," I said.

"She's always been a good one. Shame she's not interested in fellas."

"Yup."

"Her grandpa would be proud of her."

"I forgot you knew Jack, you old geezer."

"Bite your tongue, whippersnapper."

I chuckled and opened the ammo barrel.

An hour and a half later I was very glad I'd filled up the ammo bins for the minis.

"You see the one on the left?" Pop asked.

"I got him, Pop."

The left minigun began spitting fire as I sent a hail of bullets into the windshield of the old Galahad pickup. There were four guys in the back and bullets peppered Charlene until the heavy glass finally succumbed to the steady fire. The driver lurched and the truck swerved and plowed through the guard rail.

I looked out the side window and saw the truck rolling down Clinch Mountain.

"Incoming!" I yelled as I turned back to the road.

Pop jerked the wheel and barely got out of the way of the incoming rocket that blasted past us and impacted the other pickup that was right behind us. It was a Micro which didn't have the armor that a Galahad carried.

The explosion sent it tumbling after the other.

My target reticule went green, and I launched the right front rocket. They weren't as adept behind the wheel as Pop, so the rocket impacted the front of the last vehicle. The Raketen was a tough van, but it couldn't take a direct hit from a rocket to the windshield even with the armored glass. The explosion sent the glass into the interior like so much shrapnel and I didn't look inside as we drove by the flaming wreckage.

"Looks like you were right, Pop. They're still bent out of shape."

"They should've known better than take on Charlene," he said. "They may not have been locals. Keep your eyes peeled. If raiders moved into the area, we're gonna need to report it to the Regulators. Whether they have problems with the Jeffersons or not, they can't let raiders move in."

"Gotcha."

"By the way, that was good shootin', kid."

"If you take out the driver, it usually takes the whole vehicle out of action."

"You need to remember that," he said. "It's a lesson they learned in the arena too. Ginger's going to be their target more times than not."

"Gonna have to be careful. I just wish I knew what vehicles we'd be usin' so I can study up on it a little."

"Yeah, the pricks keep that secret until just before the match this time around. They're gonna use audience votes to pick who gets to choose first for their car."

"Have I told you how much I hate the autoduel racket?"

"Not in the last thirty minutes, anyway."

I laughed.

Pop looked at me a moment and back at the road. "You'll be good at it, though."

"Hmph," I grunted as I realized what he meant. I had just killed at least twelve men and felt little remorse for it.

They'd come to kill us and failed. I felt little pity for them. Was I every bit the monster they wanted me to be on TV?

Perhaps.

Chapter 17

"We have some breaking news on our Amateur Night teams, Gavin."

"What sort of news, Ellen?"

"Oh, we've got a report of an altercation on Highway 25 involving a member of one of our prospective teams at the end of the month."

"Do tell!"

"None other than the I-75 Butcher, Gavin! And he's been at it again! Regulator Chief Murphy has posted an official report that a band of raiders had moved into the small community of Thorn Hill, terrorizing the locals and causing a great deal of trouble. Unfortunately for them, they decided to attack travelers on their way to Morristown. They went for, you guessed it, Jake Turner, the Butcher himself!

"Four well-armed vehicles are nothing but flaming wreckage on the roads across Clinch Mountain and his body count has risen by ten bodies found at the scene and probably more after the search of the ravine where the third wreck was located!"

"You heard it right here folks! In two more weeks you can see it for yourselves when—"

"Seriously?" I asked as I picked up the remote and shut the TV off.

"You and Mister Turner got jumped on the mountain?" Ginger asked. "You didn't bother to tell me?"

"Wish you'd call me Larry, girl," Pop's voice came from the kitchen. "Mister Turner sounds old."

"You are old, Pop," I said.

"But you don't have to keep remindin' me."

"I'll call you Larry when you stop calling me girl," she said.

I heard him chuckling as he went out the door.

"And that brings me back to the question," she said. "You didn't bother to tell me? Were you going to say anything?"

I shrugged.

"You're even worse now than you were before you left, Jake Turner!" She stood and scowled at me.

"What?"

She let out a long breath. "I'm going home."

"You gonna come by here in the mornin' so we can head out for Knoxville?"

"I'm not riding that bike."

"You don't have to worry about that. Charlie is sendin' someone to pick us up. I reckon she was a little pissed about that bit on Clinch Mountain. She said somethin' about havin' too much money invested to let me get my fool head blown off."

"Until it can be done on screen, I imagine."

"That's about what I figured too. God forbid I go out and get killed when no one's watchin' it."

"Maybe I should just stay here tonight. There's nobody at home."

"That's fine," I said stepping out the door. "I'm goin' to feed the cow."

Pop stepped in as I went out. I stopped on the front porch and picked up a jar of his whiskey that sat on the rail.

"He's so cold now Mister Turner." I heard her through the door that wasn't quite shut. "What happened to him out there?"

"Girl, he ain't the same boy who left here with a broken heart. That boy would be useless to you where you're going. He went through something out there and it made him the man he is. I barely reacted to that attack by the time he was already laying into them with the minis. He took out the first car before I even knew they were there. It was a damn good trap, but he saw it and acted. That's the man you need out there where you're goin'. Not some fool kid who ran off to die."

"He can't be both?"

"Maybe someday. But you better follow his lead out there if you want to live through it. I 'bout guarantee the safest place to be is goin' to be right behind him. If you want to know what happened, you'll have to ask him yourself."

I took a gulp from the fire water in the jar and walked to the barn.

He was right. They didn't need Jake Turner, they needed the I-75 Butcher, the monster I had become. They needed the killer.

Pop was sitting in the kitchen with a jar on the table in front of him when I came back inside. Ginger was nowhere to be seen.

"Thought you quit drinkin', Pop."

"Been tryin' to decide if I should take it back up."

I picked up the jar. "Nope. I'll take care of that decision for you." I went to the fridge and put the jar inside.

"Hmph," he grunted.

"She gone to bed?"

He pointed toward the back of the house. "Spare bedroom."

I nodded.

"You should tell her what happened."

"Why? It would just hurt her more."

"She's got no idea what's about to happen, kid."

"I don't think anyone does. This race across country, I don't think we'll be able to dodge that if we can win the entry. Did you know they already plan to post the route?"

"What?"

"I've watched more news than I like lately," I said. "They're really doublin' down on that whole I-75 Butcher thing. But I saw that they plan to release the routes close to a month before the run."

"Jesus."

"I know, right? There's goin' to be a lot of new groups movin' into the country lookin' to get famous. I reckon the networks are plannin' some spectacular deaths for us."

"Designated routes?"

"That's what I'm hearin'."

"So everyone knows where you are and when you'll be there."

"That's about the gist of it."

"I picked a bad time to quit drinkin'."

"Guess it's a good thing I didn't." I went back to the fridge and took the jar back out. "Night, Pop."

Chapter 18

"Looks like the last team for Amateur Night has been released, Ellen."

"Don't leave me in suspense, Gavin. Who is it?"

"Big Bill's Dine and Dash has sponsored one of their own teams in this one. Let me see if you recognize either of these. Annabelle Axe and Fiona Fire."

"Those are some pretty recognizable names, Dan. I seem to remember an Amateur Night last year …"

"That's right, fans! Team Toxic is back for more! I guess they want a piece of the Dead Man's Run!"

"More likely, they want that Gold Cross package. That's one hell of a prize to win. What would you do for immortality?"

"As close to immortality as you can get," he said. "Platinum is a lifetime guarantee. A hundred-year contract with Gold Cross. You can bet, fans, this is one of the biggest pulls to get these entrants to come out of the woodwork."

"My question is 'Why just take entrants from amateurs,' Dan?"

"That's a good question, Ellen. Some of the other cities are bringing in veterans to do their legs of the Run. Why has TTA decided it will only accept amateurs?"

"My sources say it was a good choice," she said. "The ratings went through the roof after last month's Amateur Night. And next week's event promises to be even more popular."

I would have loved to switch off the television, but I was sitting in the hotel bar, and they frown on a person just shutting the thing off.

I threw back the tumbler of whiskey and it burned going down. Pop's was better.

Charlie had shown up in a helicopter to bring us to the city. I'd never ridden in a chopper, and it was interesting. It was only about forty miles away, but she wasn't prepared to risk us on even a short trip. She'd been pissed after the thing in Thorn Hill.

I tuned out the talking heads on the TV and tapped my glass when the bartender made her rounds. She refilled my glass.

"You're that guy on the vids, the I-75 Butcher."

I drained my glass and tapped it again.

She poured another. "The group at the end of the bar asked. I'm not sure of their motivation."

I looked down the bar to see who she was talking about. Three guys and two girls were conversing, but I saw two of the men look my way during the talking. They tried to be low key about it, but I caught it.

"Don't know any butchers, I'm completely vegetarian."

She snorted. "I'll give them my professional opinion that there's no way the Butcher could be a vegetarian."

I chuckled as she moved back down the bar. I took another drink from the tumbler. They could do a lot with algae, but you couldn't beat good corn liquor. The good thing about the algae was the price. It was abundant so it wasn't expensive. Pop's liquor was a lot rarer. He could get a hundred and fifty bucks for a jar. You didn't see much of that in Knoxville since corn was such a rarity. Pop had several types of hooch, but the corn liquor was the most popular.

Technically most of the population was vegetarian. Most "meat" was plant based anyway. But out in the country, there was more real meat than what you could find in the cities. It was still there but only the rich could afford it. The mule steaks Pop had fixed had been great and probably could have padded his pocket quite nicely if he'd put them in the cooler and brought them to Knoxville.

"Mule was an asshole," I muttered. "Deserved to get eaten."

One of the reasons the Paynes were as wealthy as they were was the herd of cattle they raised. Beef was in high demand and there wasn't near the supply to cover it. Especially in the "Lawless Lands" of Tennessee.

I wondered how much longer it would be before TTA managed to change that status. They were the big dogs in all three major cities, Knoxville, Chattanooga, and Memphis. Nashville was another matter altogether. The city had collapsed during the Bad Times, and it never recovered. It was a dead city now. Only thing found in Nashville anymore was ruin.

My thoughts were interrupted as the biggest of the three guys at the end of the bar drained his glass and walked my direction.

"Shit," I muttered.

I would have been skeptical if it was the smallest one.

I let out a long breath as he stopped about three feet from me.

"Jake Turner?"

I turned around ready for anything, my hand lay close to the hand cannon on my side. Ready for anything except what he did.

He held out a magazine. "Would you sign my AADA Weekly?"

I was confused.

"I mean, if you don't want to…"

"Um… Sure, I guess."

"Thanks, man!" He placed the magazine on the bar and pulled a pen from his pocket. "This is gonna be awesome! We're looking forward to next Friday. Just a heads up though, you better watch out for Toxic. They're meaner than hell."

I signed the front of the magazine feeling a little weird. "We'll keep an eye out for 'em."

"Is your driver here too?"

"She is. Up in her room."

"I wonder if I could manage to get her autograph too."

"I can ask, I guess." I pulled my cell phone from my pocket and called hers. "Hey Gin, there's some folks down in the bar would like your autograph."

"Bullshit," she answered.

"Seriously," I said.

I hung up. "She said she'll be down in a couple minutes."

The whole thing felt surreal, but Ginger walked into the bar after about fifteen minutes. The guy had gone back over to his friends and was showing off the magazine by then.

She stopped beside me. "You were kidding, right? Just tired of drinking alone?"

I shook my head. "I drink alone all the time. Kids at the end of the bar wanted an autograph."

She looked toward them. "I'll be damned."

"That's what I said. Come on and meet our first fans." I stood and walked down the bar. "Ginger, this is Jackson Louderman."

I nodded toward the big guy. "Jackson, this is Ginger Yates."

He stood up with a huge grin. "I've seen all your races!"

"You've been to Tazewell?"

"No, ma'am. I watched the vids after you guys were sponsored. You're a top notch driver."

We sat in the two stools beside them.

I watched, mostly, as Ginger signed the magazine and spent the whole evening regaling them with stories about racing. I watched and I drank. I wasn't about to start telling stories about what I had done to qualify as a gunner. The only time the subject came up, Ginger handily steered the conversation in a different direction with a tale of racing.

I left the group about midnight and returned to my room. I hadn't done much socializing in the last six years, and it was hard. It was difficult to enjoy the company of others. Most of the people I associated with in those six years died in front of me and came back as clones. Some of them multiple times.

Chapter 19

"One more day, race fans!" The radio woke me up. "Tomorrow is Amateur Night, and we'll see who the next entrant into Dead Man's Run will be!!"

I slammed my hand down on the top of the alarm and it shut off.

"Thought that was set to the ringer," I muttered.

It seemed like every time a radio or TV was on it was talking about tomorrow's arena duel. I was already sick of it, but I knew there was so much more to come. If we managed to win tomorrow, we would be under the public eye for a long time. But she would have the Gold Cross package and that was what we were here for.

I went to the bathroom and took a shower. Today we would get our first look at the track for tomorrow. And we would get to see what cars we would be using. We would have one night to study the equipment and the weapons as well as strategize how to use the track.

It wasn't enough time, but it would have to do. My time in the Road Guard had taught me to use any kind of weapons available. I still hoped they would give us something I was familiar with.

As I reached into the hotel closet for the uniform, the door to the adjoining room opened and I heard a gasp.

"Oh… God…" Her voice was barely a whisper. "Jesus, what happened to you out there?"

I stopped moving, unsure what I could say. The scars on my back were unmistakable. Three days they'd tortured me before I escaped.

I closed my eyes, remembering a better time, as her hands touched my back.

"I'm so sorry, Jake."

I took a deep breath. "That's not on you. That's mine."

She wrapped her arms around my ribs, and I could feel her face against my back. I turned around and she rested her head on my chest. I wrapped my arms around her, and she sobbed.

We stayed that way for some time before she stepped back and gasped again at the jagged scar across my chest.

"Mister Turner said it was bad," she said and sniffed. Her eyes were red. "This is what he was talking about isn't it?"

"Yeah," I said. "He calls it a crucible. I guess that's accurate enough."

"This is why you act like you're a monster?"

"No. It's what I did after I escaped. I killed 'em, Gin. Every damned one of 'em."

"They were torturing you," she said.

"I could have escaped into the night, Gin. The way was open, and it would have been easy. But that's not what I did. I stormed through that camp with a powerful hate in me. I didn't leave any of them alive."

Her face was pale.

"Gin, you can't kill that many people and consider yourself anything other than what I am. I'm a killer and I'm very good at it."

"How—"

"How many? That's what everyone asks."

"I didn't mean that to come out."

"It's a normal reaction," I said. "After a while you tend to lose count."

"Jesus," she whispered.

"Go get ready," I said. "We have to be down in the lobby in twenty minutes."

She slowly moved away and went back through the door.

You don't tend to lose count. I knew there were fifty-eight souls I had personally sent to whatever afterlife that awaited us. And twelve more that Pop and I had sent there on Clinch Mountain. Seventy lives I was responsible for ending. In one way or another. I had a feeling there would be a lot more before this was through.

Twenty minutes later we exited the lobby in our racing suits. They were tight-fitting but surprisingly comfortable black body suits with red designs. I couldn't help but think the design looked like blood spatter. It was probably designed just for that effect. I also couldn't help but notice Ginger. She always looked amazing, and the suit only added to it.

Ginger was quiet as we sat in the back seat of the sedan. I caught a few looks in my direction from her and I could see the worry writ large on her face. I had been keeping the details of my past away from her because of this very thing. But in the event we were about to be a part of, she probably needed to know my past as well as I needed to know hers.

"If you really want to know what happened, Gin, I'll tell you everything. I should have already done that. We need to know each other so we can trust each other again."

"Agreed," she said. "When we get back tonight."

I nodded.

We remained quiet all the way to Neyland Stadium where crowds were already forming. Floating camera drones were all over the place and dozens of microphone carrying reporters lined the side of the large ramp into the stadium.

Years ago Neyland was just used for football, then deathball once the laws allowed blood sports. It was still a massive deathball stadium, but it was also the place we would be introduced to the public and shown what we would be operating in tomorrow's Amateur Night.

There were cheers as Ginger got out of the car and I followed. We both stood with our mouths hanging open for a moment. Seeing crowds of people on television was a whole different thing. Ginger raised her hand and waved. The crowd of people lining the ramp exploded in applause.

She turned to me with her face beaming. Last time I saw that was when she had won that last race. Just before she saw me.

I looked around and sighed.

Charlie stepped between us and locked her arms in ours. "Your future awaits."

We walked up the ramp just like that with cameras flashing and news drones overhead. It was insane.

At the top of the ramp we entered massive glass doors and entered a crowded lobby. Cheers echoed from the walls, and I swallowed. They had warned me what to expect but the reality of it was completely different.

Ginger waved and the crowd cheered again.

"You could smile," Charlie said.

I grimaced and continued walking.

Chapter 20

""Today we get to see what our competitors will get to use in tomorrow's event, Ellen, and TTA really dug deep to find these classics!"

"Gavin, those look like six matching Hudson Hammers! We haven't seen any of these running the tracks in a while!"

"That's right Ellen. The Hudson Hammer is an old car but it's pure gold. And those aren't exactly matching Hammers either. Each of these babies is sporting a different loadout of weapons and we're going to do a live poll of the audience to see who will get to choose their car first!"

The talking heads on the big screen were the same ones who did the announcements for Amateur Night, and I was beginning to get used to them. I'd heard a lot of their spiel over the last month. I stood alongside of Ginger and focused on the cars. The first had a pair of recoilless rifles jutting from the front ports and a flamethrower on the turret. The Hammer came standard with a turret and all six of the cars had them. The second looked like a heavy caliber single shot but I didn't see a front weapon. Third had two recoilless in the front gun ports and a Vulcan mini gun on the turret. Fourth was another flamethrower. Fifth was another with a single-shot on the turret but it also had the pair of recoilless on the front. And the sixth had the recoilless in two front ports with another Vulcan.

"I'm guessin' the one with the single weapon has somethin' in the back. Rockets or mines or somethin'."

"Probably," Ginger said. "I wonder what they have for a power plant."

"Ellen, these vehicles have been meticulously gone over to have the same weight to power ratio so that they will be evenly matched. Even the weight of the driver and gunner will be accounted for. The only difference will be the weapon load out."

"That should make for an interesting event, Gavin!"

"I guess that answers that," Ginger said.

"And now we'll go to the polls! We have given every person in the stands today a chance to choose who gets to pick their vehicle first! The tablet in front of you has the names of our six teams and you will need to enter them in the order you would like to see. You have three minutes to make your decisions and we will tally the votes!"

The next three minutes seemed to stretch on forever.

"Alright, race fans! The tally is in, and our first team is, not unexpectedly, returning winners of Amateur Night, Toxic!"

"I'm guessin', with their reputation, they'll go for a flame thrower," I said. "It's a damned ugly weapon."

The two women strode forward with fists in the air, screaming to the audience. Their suits were form-fitting like ours, but they wore their signature jackets over them. Annabelle Axe wore a black leather jacket with metal studs that matched the piercings on her face. Fiona Fire wore a green leather jacket with similar studs. On the back of both jackets was the word Toxic.

They made the rounds of the vehicles, but they weren't overly interested. It was a show for the audience when they paused at each vehicle. The crowd would cheer at each one, but they really went wild when the women stopped at the first flame thrower.

"Try not to look so disgusted, Jake." Charlie stood behind us. "It doesn't look good on camera."

"Whatever," I muttered.

"And our toxic ladies have chosen car number one!"

"Our second team," Ellen said, "is none other than Fountain City's own, Orange Crush! The Youngs will get to choose the next car!"

Kaleb and Jasmine Young moved forward in a dance step. Their jumpsuits were orange, of course. They went straight for the first Vulcan.

"Probably the best weapon load out," I said.

"Probably."

"Orange Crush is in car number three!" Gavin yelled and the crowd cheered again.

"Next are the terror of the freeways, the Blacktop Butchers!"

We walked calmly down to the cars, and I went to number two. It was indeed a mine layer, which was a lot lighter than the weapon load outs on the other vehicles. To compensate there was added armor to the driver side of the car.

I pointed to the extra plate. "This is the one."

"Are you sure?"

"Weapon load out is less, but it has extra armor and I'm all for that."

"Alright then."

We moved to the front of the car and stood.

Annabelle Axe snickered. "Gonna roast you alive, butcher."

I turned my head toward them with a dead look. Her eye twitched.

I turned back to the front.

"You'll have to catch us first," Ginger said with a grin. "Good luck with that."

"Gonna be a shame to kill such a pretty plaything," Fiona said with a sneer. "You'd make a fine pet."

"You're looking disgusted again," Ginger whispered.

"I hate this shit."

"They can't hurt what they can't catch."

"True enough," I said.

"Next we have the Maryville Madmen!"

Two guys in purple jumpsuits and top hats, each sporting a black walking stick, pranced down to inspect the cars. They settled in front of the other Vulcan.

The Rabble Rousers in their yellow suits took the other flamethrower and the Bradyville Banshees were left with car number five.

"And there we have it, Ellen! We have our teams, and we have our cars!"

"Next, Gavin, we'll all make our way out of the big doors so they can get a first look at the track!"

We followed behind Axe and Fire toward the main gate and up the long stairs to the grandstands around the autoduel arena where we all lined up and looked down on the track.

"Standard oval," Ginger said quietly. "Obstructions in the center."

"To keep us from shooting across the arena."

"Ramps and manufactured hills in there. Looks like packed dirt so traction gets a lot worse if you go off track."

A pretty blonde walked down the line of contestants and gave each of us a pamphlet. As she handed Fiona Fire hers, Fire made a suggestive gesture with her tongue.

Camera drones circled us getting every expression and movement for the vids. One of them stopped directly in front of us and I gave it a cold dead stare while Ginger waved and smiled.

We spent half of the day in front of those cameras, parading around for the vids. I was surprised how exhausting it was. Ginger, on the other hand, reveled in it. She was always comfortable in front of the cameras at the races, so she was better adapted to it than I was.

Later, I sat in the chair in my room with a jar of Pop's whiskey.

Ginger walked in from her adjoining room and sat down on the sofa. "Time to work."

It was a long evening. We studied the information they had provided about the cars, the track, and the rules. Then we planned strategies. We were as prepared as we could be.

She turned to me and opened the jar. "Now tell me."

"What?"

"Tell me all of it."

I didn't want to talk about it, and I definitely didn't want to talk about it with her. But we needed to trust one another so I took a long drink from the jar. "You already know where it starts. I guess I'll just begin with getting to Knoxville where …"

114 | P a g e

Chapter 21

"Today is the day, boys and girls! The day we've been waiting for all month! Tonight is Amateur Night in Knoxville! Tune in early and you can see the coverage beginning with your favorite teams. Log on to our site and you can join the streams for the team you want to follow through the day and see how they prepare for this duel. Fan favorite Toxic has already begun with their familiar tour of K-town and The Orange Crush is hosting a celebration in Fountain City at The Crush. Right off of I-640. Everyone is welcome! Come on out and—"

I turned off the TV and opened the door to find cameras waiting outside of our rooms. Drones floated close to the ceiling in the hallway.

"They'll be present from here on out," Charlie said from my left where she had been waiting. "Except for inside your rooms. Larry is on his way in on the chopper and wants to have lunch with you before the event this evening. I've made sure there won't be any cameras present for that."

"Last meal, huh?"

She motioned for me to step back inside the room.

When the door closed behind us she said, "I certainly hope not. Favor or not, I wouldn't sponsor someone I didn't think could win. I've never seen anyone who could drive any better than your girl. You're the joker in the deck, the wild card. I saw what you and Larry did on the mountain and, more importantly, I heard what he said happened. He doesn't talk about his past much, but he spent some time in Bowling Green around the circuit. He says you're a natural gunner. Better than he ever was."

"Pops was a gunner?"

She chuckled. "Yeah, kid. He was a gunner alright, it's not a coincidence he married my sister. We've been autoduelling for generations."

"He never said anything."

"That's part of the job, kid. Nondisclosure agreements are common in the industry. But I'm the holder of that agreement now, so I can choose who knows about it. He trusts you so I do too."

"How was he a gunner and the press didn't find him?"

"He was Jeremiah Hood."

"You're shittin' me. I don't like the autoduelling world and even I've heard of the Hoods. If he was Jeremiah, who was Kelly? Was my grandma a Hood?" I paused a moment. "No, you were Kelly Hood. He named his car after you and not Gran."

The Hoods were well known in their day. No one knew how many "Hoods" there had been over the years, but the team had been around for twenty years or so.

"We always had a thing for each other," she said. "But I was married, and he was dating my sister, so nothing ever came of it. We played our roles for four years. Almost died several times. Then the next 'Hoods' were hired, and the brand went on. He bought some acreage in the hills, and I started managing under my original name."

I took a moment to let it sink in before speaking. "Was my dad a gunner?"

"Nope." She took the jar of shine from the dresser top and unscrewed the lid. "Larry said Tyler was a hell of a fighter, but he burned hot as the sun. He was all fury. Larry said you were cold as ice when you took out those raiders on the mountain. Said you were already shooting before he could even react to the first vehicle. He was a hell of a gunner when we worked the Arenas. That says all I need to hear to put you in a car."

"I was the one with the sensor HUD."

"Do you think he didn't have his HUD on as well?"

"He never said anything."

"That's Larry. Would you have driven while someone else controlled the sensors?"

I chuckled. "True enough."

"I can do that, but I was a driver. He was a gunner. There's no way he doesn't have his HUD active."

"Why are you telling me this, now?"

"It's safe to talk about it since the Hoods retired almost five years ago, for one. Secondly, you probably won't get a chance to talk about it at lunch. The cameras shouldn't be there but there's no guarantee. The press are a tenacious bunch. Thirdly, he wanted you to know before you go out there and he didn't get the chance to tell you himself. Once I sponsored you, there was no telling who was listening. Even out in the backwoods."

"I knew Pop was from somewhere else, but I never expected this. He hates the whole thing so much, I was surprised it was his suggestion to do it. We never watched it on the vids when I was a kid."

"He learned to hate it while we were the Hoods. He got as far away from it as he could while I dove in head first. I loved to drive, and I loved the game."

"Why did you step down?"

"I wouldn't trust another gunner after Larry kept me alive for those four years. That's the gunner's job, Jake. That's your job. You keep your team alive. That's your mission out there today. I've seen her races. If you keep that girl alive, she'll drive the wheels off anything she's in and leave everyone wondering what hit them. Can you do that?"

"Yes ma'am."

"Then you two can make one hell of a team out there."

"We'll do our best, ma'am."

"Enough with the ma'am shit, Jake. We're all just car warriors. Call me Charlie."

I nodded.

"Now let's see about getting your girl moving so we can do the whole public appearance thing before meeting Larry."

There was a light knock at the door separating the two rooms and Ginger stuck her head inside the room. "Did you know the hall is full of stupid camera drones?"

She saw Charlie sitting in the chair beside the window. "Oh, hey Miss Graven. I guess you already know then."

"That's what you need to expect from this point forward. It'll be worse when you win this thing tonight. You ready for that, girl?"

"Yes ma'am."

Charlie sighed.

"What?"

"You're as bad as he is. Ma'am, sir, missus…"

I chuckled.

"Just like I told Mister Turner, when you all quit calling me girl, I'll think about the mister and missus thing."

Charlie cocked her head to the side a fraction and thought a moment. Then she started laughing. "You're gonna be gold on the cameras, girl. Every one of those teams out there are playing a persona they've built for the vids. I swear, all you need is to be yourself. If not for this lump over here, I'd have to name your team the Hometown Honeys or something."

Ginger looked at me. "It'd be hard to call him that, now, wouldn't it?"

I grunted.

"No truer words have ever been spoken, girl."

"I thought you were sayin' somethin' about gettin' this thing rollin', ma'am," I said.

"Be careful or I'll change the name to the Hometown Honey and the Killbilly."

Ginger snorted and sat on the bed. "I could get behind that."

"No doubt," I said.

"Killbilly." She giggled.

It was a sound I hadn't heard for six years, and I missed it.

Chapter 22

Welcome to Amateur Night in Knoxville! For those of you new to us, the rules are simple. Three laps around the track before our teams' weapons go live! Then our gunners can engage! All the cars are equal in power and weight, with the drivers and gunners included, so this is going to be one hell of a race even before the weapons go live!"

The talking head floating above the arena was loud enough for us to hear in the car. Ginger was strapped into her seat, gripping the wheel to keep her right hand from shaking and I had the weapon controls all around me in the gunner chair. My HUD wasn't even live yet.

"I have an idea," I said.

"What's that?"

"These mines have a manual release. If I lose about a hundred pounds, how much faster can you run this? Fast enough to get our weapons live before any of theirs?"

"Pretty sure I can."

"Then I need you to run the first lap on the outside. If it works and they set off the mines, I want to get the left side of the cars. Might take out one of those flame throwers or damage the gunner controls."

"Why not try for the fronts since all of them have those weapons?"

"The tanks for the flame throwers are right behind the gunner chair. The only use for a flamethrower in something like this is to kill the driver and gunner. The cars are made to take that heat, we're not. I would love to remove those from the fight if we can."

"Gotcha. I'll run the outside, but I'll lose a little time doing it."

"Will the weight loss make it up?"

"It should."

I saw the light stand turn orange. "Looks like it's about to start. You ready to race?"

"I'm always ready to race."

The green light flashed, and Ginger floored it, launching the car forward hard enough to jerk my head back into the headrest. I almost missed the first drop because we were going so fast. Just before reaching the ramp where the Orange Crush team had hit the track, I pulled the lever and dropped the first mine.

We had been on ramp four. I dropped another mine at ramp six where the Bradyville Banshees had been. Then Ginger took the curve with the back of the car sliding toward the outer rail.

"They call this drifting," she said.

Whatever they called it, it gained any ground we might have lost with running on the outside. I dropped the mine at ramp one where the Maryville Madmen started and two others at ramp two and three where Toxic and the Rabble Rousers started.

"Reckon that's it," I said. "Do your thing."

"Hold on to your lug nuts!"

I thought she had taken the first turn fast. This time I was almost completely sideways as we rounded the turn before she pulled the car back straight and shot forward again. We had gained a car length on the Crush.

I watched the car in front of us as it got closer and the one behind us get further behind. Ginger drifted around the next curve and gained even more. She was close to the inside, and I dropped another mine at ramp two and three.

"More?"

"I really want those flamethrowers out of this."

"Agreed. Want to drop the others on the next one?"

"Probably need to keep a couple in case we need them."

"Okay."

We rounded the next curve to pass our starting point.

"One more lap," she said.

She kept inching forward toward the orange car in front of us. The weight drop helped on the straightaways and Ginger's demonic driving brought us ever closer on the turns.

"They're on the outside," I said. "I'm takin' out that front left tire. You peg that rear fender, and we might get lucky."

"Gotcha."

My HUD lit up and I brought the turret around and put three shots into the front tire which couldn't take the punishment. The front of the car dropped, and Ginger hit the fender on the rear.

The car started sideways, and Ginger floored it. They slid sideways across the mine I had dropped, and the left side of the car lifted with the explosion to send it rolling down the track.

"With luck, they're out of it," I said as I lined the turret on the Banshees just as the mine exploded on their right side.

They shot to the left and made it behind one of the hills in the center of the track before I could hit them more than once. My shot was at their power plant, but I wasn't sure if it had hit or not.

We streaked around the track at high speed, my HUD tracking where the others were. The Banshees and the

Madmen were off the track in the center of the dirt embankments, but the Rabble Rousers and Toxic weren't.

"Oh my god…" Ginger gasped as we rounded the curve.

"Oh, hell no…"

"That was one slick move by the Butchers, ladies and gentlemen! The Orange Crush are in trouble! Aaaand they're on their roof and out of this one, fans. Out of it without firing a shot!"

The arena rocked with multiple mines. "Looks like everyone has taken damage from the Butchers' little trap. The double R and Toxic seem to have lost most of the armored glass. Wait a minute! What's this? Rabble Rousers just opened fire on the Crush with the flamethrower! This is as dirty as it gets… Oh, no! Toxic has joined them! This looks like the last race for the Crush, ladies and gents!"

The crowd seemed to be holding their breath.

"Here come the Butchers! Are they going to join…" The crowd went wild. "What was that? Was that a grenade?"

The arena shook with the explosion as the grenade went off. "Toxic is out! Toxic is done! Toxic is dead!"

I raised the window just before the grenade went off. Our car lurched as they exploded in a ball of fire. I was already swinging the turret around and fired directly into the driver side window of the Rabble Rousers. I triggered the turret four times and one of them must have hit the napalm tanks because the inside of their car looked like I was staring straight into hell.

"Jesus…"

"Pop said to show mercy when you can," I said. "And be ruthless when you need to. They didn't deserve mercy."

The Banshees rounded the curve as we surged forward.

They opened fire on the rear of our car as soon as they reached range.

I spun the turret and sent my last three shots into the front of their car.

"We can't take much more fire! Brake hard and throttle when I say!"

She didn't even hesitate, and the Banshees hit the back of our car.

The Hudson Hammer is designed with a low front so it can be used to flip other cars. As the rear of our car rose up onto the hood of the Banshees I dropped the last two mines.

"Now!"

Ginger floored it and the mines exploded right on top of their power plant, sending us forward hard enough to plant us both into our seats. My HUD showed all of the cars were still except ours.

Something was scraping and the throttle didn't give us much speed, but Ginger drove down the victory ramp under our own power. Even if we were dragging the back half of the car on the pavement.

"Glad you kept those mines," Ginger said shakily. "I hope they're okay."

"Should have just taken out the power plant."

"I mean the Crush. I can't believe they were doing that. Why would they do that? They were out."

"Pop said some people were in this for the money. Others? Well, others are just evil."

"I hate this."

"Me too."

126 | Page

"Pop said some people were in this for the money. Others? Well, others are just evil."

"I hate this."

"Me too."

Chapter 23

"What do you think of your victory tonight?" the blonde anchor asked.

"What do I think? I think I'm just glad the Youngs are okay." Ginger pointed back toward the track. "Why in the world were they attacking someone that was already out of the race? They were trying to kill that couple and I think it's just evil."

"Wasn't your gunner's action just as violent?"

"It damn sure was violent. Someone gave us some advice before this event. He said be merciful when you can, these folks are trying to make a living just like anyone else. But when you can't you need to be ruthless. Both of those teams were truly evil. They got what they deserved."

"I wonder how you'll feel after a few years on the circuit. Will you still feel the same? How long can you hold on to your innocence?"

"I hope I feel the same as I do right now. There's a right and there's a wrong to every action. I hope I can see that difference until the day I die."

"Do you have anything to add, Mister Turner?"

"She covered it pretty well," I said.

"But does she really know who her partner is? Does she know the I-75 Butcher? What about all of those bodies in your past Mister Tur…"

I turned the television off.

"You can't do that!"

The voice came from behind me, and I turned to find the man who had complained reaching for me. He stopped as I turned and he stepped back, bumping into one of his friends.

"Oh shit, you're him."

"And I think I've had enough of that crap for the day. Is that alright with you?"

"Y…yeah. Sure thing."

I looked over his shoulder at the pair of camera drones.

"I'll take that bottle to go if you don't mind," I said to the bartender. "Add it to my room."

"Do you need anything else, Mister Turner?" She gave me a small smile. "Anything at all."

"Just the bottle tonight."

She nodded and handed me the whiskey with a pout.

I chuckled and made my way through the crowded hotel bar. The camera drones followed me. They tried to enter the elevator with me, but I pushed them both out as the door closed.

"You can fly," I muttered. "Take the scenic route."

The elevator passed my floor.

"Shit."

It opened on the forty-second floor where a pretty girl waited.

"Mister Turner."

"Uh… yeah."

"Your room is this way, sir." She motioned for me to follow as she walked down the hall. "You are in suite forty-two-oh-two. Your teammate is in forty-two-oh-three, across the hall. Camera drones will not be permitted on this level, sir."

I nodded and took the key fob she held out to me as we reached the door. "Thank you."

"Is there anything else you require, sir? My job is to provide for your needs."

"My needs?"

"Many racers, after a duel, need … certain things."

I let out a slow breath. "I'm fine. All I need is a bath and to drink this bottle so I can sleep."

"As you wish."

I wasn't sure if it was relief I saw in her eyes or not, her face had remained impassive, but I was pretty sure about what I had been offered. I was curious why she was offering if she didn't want to, but that lasted only an instant. TTA was funding our amenities now. The bartender had genuinely offered herself while this girl had been ordered to.

"Just another thing to hate about this," I muttered as I entered my suite.

"Talking to yourself?"

Ginger stood behind the bar located on the far side of the room. There was a couch and several comfortable chairs between the door and the bar. To the left was a small kitchenette and a door on the right.

She pointed at the bottle of whiskey. "You drinking that crap? No wonder you're talking to yourself."

"It was what they had in the bar."

"How were you even in the bar? People keep wanting to grab me in there and get pictures and stuff."

"You're pretty. They want pictures with you." I took a long pull from the bottle. "They mostly run away from me."

"What the hell happened? Yesterday we had two or three people who wanted to be around us. Today there was a guy waiting at the elevator for me. He said he was there to fill my needs. This is crazy."

"I know, same here."

"He propositioned you too?"

I snorted and whiskey burned my nose.

She giggled. "I saw that pretty girl at the elevator waiting for you. Why did you turn her down?"

I sat in one of the chairs as Ginger poured herself a glass of Scotch. The bottle probably cost as much as I made in a year with the road crews. "She didn't want to. She was ordered to. Which brings me back to the part where I was talkin' to myself. Just somethin' else I hate about this whole thing. At least, tomorrow we can go sign the contracts and get you over to Gold Cross."

There was a knock on the door and Ginger crossed the room to open it.

"Missus Graven."

Charlie rolled her eyes and Ginger giggled again.

Pop followed Charlie into the room.

"Hey, kid." He placed a box on the coffee table in front of the couch. "Get rid of that swill, son. I brought you somethin' else."

"Damn, Pop. A whole case?"

"Tryin' to soften the blow." He sat down in the other chair.

I drew a long breath. "What?"

"TTA is givin' Charlie grief over that I-75 Butcher thing. They're talkin' bout filin' charges, son."

"Why's he smiling?" Charlie asked. "You're not supposed to be smiling. This is serious. They can decline your contract for the Run. What's with the shit eating grin?"

"Nothin'." I sat the bottle down and pulled a jar from the box. I unscrewed the top and took a long drink. "They can't use a rumor if they file charges. They'll have to release the interview they did with me and the lie detector tests."

"What's that got to do with it?" Ginger asked.

Charlie sat on the couch with a growing smile. "Honey, if they press charges, we can use those to show the truth. I have connections outside of the lawless lands. Let me make a few calls and see what else we can add."

"Oh…"

Chapter 24

The room we were sitting in wasn't like any courtroom I'd ever seen. The only people physically present were the judge, a couple of lawyers, and me. Others were present as virtual avatars.

"Official charges were brought against my client, sir, that are provably erroneous," the defense attorney said. "Evidence provided by Leviticus Industries will be made available as necessary. Being the sole survivor the client is the only remaining witness and, as we all know, viewing of another individual's Gold Cross upload is impossible. We have discovered through the provided items another source to prove my client's innocence. The post-interview was accompanied with a very thorough lie detection process that we have provided. As you may or may not be aware this is the third sort of event my client has been involved in."

"Three murders?" The judge looked at me with a furrowed brow.

"Three events, your honor."

"And you have video of these occurrences?"

"We have been provided with evidence gained from satellite surveillance of a group of individuals that were involved in the first event along with partial coverage of the second."

"I think I will need to view it personally considering the seriousness of the charges filed against your defendant."

"The files will be provided immediately, your honor."

"Then we're adjourned until tomorrow at ten, after I've seen this footage. The defendant will remain on the grounds of his hotel until the matter is settled."

I stood with the others as the judge rose to leave.

"What is he going to see in that file?"

I turned to the defense attorney. "The truth."

He grimaced.

"Is he going to see a mass murderer? What, exactly, am I to expect when we come back tomorrow?"

"I reckon you can expect that guy to decide my future. I never worked for any raiders which is what I am being charged with and he'll see that, sure enough. You want to know more? Ask him tomorrow."

"You can't just answer the question?"

"I did." I walked away from him.

He was irritating. This is what I'd been wanting to do since they took me into the office and grilled me months ago. Provide the lie detector interview and just leave me alone.

I sat down at the defendant's seat as the two lawyers carried on a short conversation about coffee shops near the court house. They would be at one another's throats in the courtroom and go have coffee together afterwards.

"Lawyers," I muttered.

"All rise for the honorable Judge Waits."

I stood and faced the door beside the witness stand.

Judge Waits entered and made his way to his chair and motioned for everyone to take a seat.

My lawyer stepped forward and the Judge held up a finger.

"You can step back Mister Fowler. One of the hardest parts of my job is to watch something like this and thank God I couldn't feel what I witnessed."

"Your honor—"

"Take a seat, Mister Dent. I do not need any more input from you or Mister Fowler at the moment."

Dent sat back at the prosecutor's table and Fowler sat down beside me.

"What the hell did he watch, Turner?"

"The truth," I said.

"To start with, the first event I had to watch happened five and a half years ago, most of which happened outside in the middle of the camp. Due to this, there was an unobstructed view in the satellite footage. I have to say that it was a travesty what happened to you, Mister Turner. A person should never have to endure what happened in that camp. Without going into graphic detail, I can say that this man was captured and tortured for two days. None of his companions survived past day one. I don't understand how, but this man refused to die."

He pointed toward me. "Then he escaped and, despite an aversion to violence that I am well known for, I witnessed the execution of twenty-six men and women that deserved that fate. It troubles me that I can say that, but it's the unvarnished truth. After watching that, I don't think there is any way in this whole misbegotten world that Jake Turner began working for anyone even remotely similar to these people."

He looked at me with a haunted look. "But I was still required to observe what was viewable of the other two events. I can't even fathom why you continued working on the road crews after that first year but there were a lot of evil people out there that would have preferred if you had quit. The second event was a year and a half after the first. It was a firefight on I-40, and I saw nothing more than a man who refused to die. The fight ended when the last of the raiders was killed by Turner and he rode one of the raider's motorcycles back to Knoxville before being hospitalized with multiple gunshot wounds.

"Again, I can see no way he was cooperating with said raiders unless they were requesting assisted suicide. If I hadn't seen what was done to Mister Turner by his earlier captors, I would say that the greatest travesty of this whole situation is that he is even here at all. Mister Turner was a road crew guard and proved himself to be very adept at the job. In the instances where the crews were killed, he proved equally adept at bringing their killers to justice.

"In my opinion, the Road Crew program is necessary, but they need more funding to protect the crews. The bias against clones makes some people think they can be treated as less than human. These people are putting their lives on the line to keep the roads drivable. Unfortunately, violence will always be an issue with the program and people capable of reciprocating that violence are a necessity as well.

"I find TTA's choice to remove Mister Turner from their employ to be egregious at best. These charges are baseless and will be dropped. Frankly, I feel that Mister Turner has a strong case if he chooses to file a counter suit against his previous employer."

He once again stared at me. "You, Mister Turner, are perhaps the most terrifying individual I have ever met. Also you, sir, are most definitely not a raider. I sincerely hope this clears any questions on the subject. You are free to go, Mister Turner. Case dismissed."

I nodded at the judge, stood up, and walked out of the courtroom without another word.

Chapter 25

"They're all about signing us up now," Ginger said.

"Tryin' to keep me from doin' a countersuit, I imagine."

"More than likely," Charlie said.

I stepped off the elevator glancing back at Charlie, and I was hit by a flying body.

Jackie Shoffner planted a kiss right on my mouth as my head came back around. Her legs wrapped around my waist.

I closed my arms around her.

"Don't get any ideas," she said with a giggle. "I'm just glad you're alive. Now put me down."

"You put yourself here."

"Yeah, but now I wanna grab that red headed demon beside you."

I lowered her lightly to the floor and she embraced Ginger.

"Special torture," I muttered.

Pop stood where he had been waiting with Jackie.

I stepped forward and stood beside him.

"You sure you wanna do this, kid?"

"Have to sign the contract to get the Gold Cross."

"I know. But you saw the contract they sent over. There ain't no getting' out of doin' this Dead Man's Run. Victory or death. There's no middle ground left."

"I know. I halfway thought we could quit at some point, but the contract is pretty detailed. No way out but the other side."

"I brought the best greaser we knew to build the car."

"You got that right," I said. "She can build anything, Ginger can drive anything, I think we're as good as we can get."

"And you can kill anything that gets in the way, kid." Pop pulled a bag from his pocket and took out a wad of tobacco. "Reckon that was one hell of a match the other night. They're all cheerin' you on back home. They had that match on at the drive-in when it happened."

"They don't even like autoduelling."

"Yeah, but you two are from Tazewell. You can bet the whole town's watchin'. Don't be surprised when you see some familiar names on the Clutch Stream."

"What's that?"

"It's the feed in the cars where you can interact with your fans."

"Shit."

He chuckled. "Son, you're about to be in a whole new world."

"Joy."

"At least she's photogenic." He pointed at Ginger. "And I guarantee she already knows what the Clutch Stream is."

We crossed the lobby with camera drones hovering near.

"Damn cameras," I muttered.

"You may as well get used to that. They'll be followin' you around all year. Then they'll be all over the place during the race."

"Don't have to like it, do I?"

"Just have to accept it," he said.

"Whatever."

Ginger strode past us with a grin on her face, waving at the cameras as they closed in on her.

"I think she actually likes it," I said.

A floating head hologram appeared beside one of the drones. "Miss Yates, would you consider a short interview?"

"Sorry, I'm on my way to sign some contracts and have to be on my way but I'll be happy to do it after all that's done. You can set something up with Miz Graven."

"Fantastic!"

The drone rose back to its normal position near the ceiling.

I stepped forward and followed Ginger and Jackie toward the hotel entrance.

"It's the one waiting at the door, sweetie." Charlie stepped in front of me and touched Ginger's shoulder. "We'll be along in a second."

She stopped in front of me and motioned for Pop to join the girls. "That girl is way too sweet for this."

"Until you get her behind the wheel of a car," I said.

"True enough. From here on out you'll be in their world. When it gets ugly, I'm depending on you to keep her alive. You understand?"

I nodded. "We did this to get her a Gold Cross but if you think I plan to watch her die, you don't really know me. I'd burn the world for her and, if rumors are true about this damned race, I may have to."

"There's that Killbilly I've heard about. That's the guy that needs to be out there. You keep him close to the surface from the second you step out that door."

"Ma'am, he's always close to the surface."

"Good. Now go sign those contracts and get your girl into the data banks. Then we can start working on what kind of car you can build." She motioned toward the door with her head.

I left the hotel to find a limo waiting outside.

"That's us."

"Damn."

"Told you. It's another world under the TTA. There's a lot more to it than just corporate power like a lot of other places. They call Tennessee the lawless lands for a reason. The Bolgeos who own it never cared much for law anyway. The higher you get in the TTA, the more dangerous it gets."

"Then why bother with that trial?"

"Even the TTA is vested in ratings. They haven't been this high in thirty years. And, right now, you and your girl are at the top of the ratings. It was in their interest for you to be proven innocent. It looks better on the vids. Next month top of the ratings will be whoever wins the next Amateur Night, but you're on top right now. That's why it's important to get these contracts done. Even the Bolgeos have to answer to the AADA when it comes to autoduelling."

"How do we know they haven't slipped something else into the contracts?"

"My lawyers are combing through them as we speak. But read them yourself when we get there if it helps. You've read what they sent. My people will bring anything that has been altered to your attention at the beginning of the meeting."

We got into the limo where Ginger, Jackie, and Pop already waited.

The signing was in the TTA building where I had met with Keller, Forth, and Trent what seemed ages ago. In reality it had only been a few months. The room we entered was much nicer with a beautiful wooden table that stretched the distance of the room. There were four chairs on each side of the table. All but three on our side of the table were filled. The one on our side was Charlie's lawyer.

There were two of them on the other side I recognized, Frank Keller and Hannah Forth.

"Good morning, Mister Turner," Keller said. He motioned toward Forth. "My associate and I are here to offer our sincere apologies after the debacle of our last meeting. TTA is happy that the matter could be settled, and your name cleared of any wrongdoing."

He gave me a small grin and winked his right eye. Keller had never supported the decision made by the other two.

"Indeed, our sincerest apologies, Mister Turner." Forth looked like she was sucking on a lemon. "The matter is settled?"

I smiled and her face paled.

"That is all we need from you two," the woman on the far right said. "You may go."

Forth stood up with a defeated air about her and Keller stood with that same small smile on his face.

I stood and shook Keller's hand. "The matter's settled as far as I'm concerned. I hate to see someone punished for someone else's bad decision."

"They always need a fall guy." He shrugged and left the room.

"Now, Mister Turner and Miss Yates, shall we get down to business? I am Stephanie Collins. I'll be going over your contract with you as you sign." She motioned toward Charlie's lawyer. "Miss Reilly has looked at the contract in depth so I will be summarizing each form. First and foremost, we will set up your platinum package with Gold Cross. You understand this is a premium service worth a great deal. As long as you complete your contract, you will retain this package for life. The stipulations to keep the package is fairly simple. Survive the race or die trying. There is no quitting. The only way out is through the other side. Do you both understand?"

I nodded and looked to my left to see Ginger nod as well.

"Then, as I said, we'll get this set up and you will have Gold Cross available when you leave this building. Next will be a standard non-disclosure agreement."

Signing the contract took several hours. The contracts with TTA and the AADA were very detailed, all the way down to what kind of car we would be allowed to build for the Dead Man's Run. Reilly made sure they were explained without the "lawyer speak" that contracts were always filled with.

My thoughts were on the vehicle we would need for this thing. Most autoduellists would be thinking about weapons. My thoughts were on armor. There would likely be a lot of people trying to kill us. More than the amount of ammo we could carry in a Division Eight vehicle.

Chapter 26

"Mister Turner," Janice greeted me as we entered the office. He was wearing a flamboyant orange kimono.

"Janice."

He laughed at Ginger's confused look and turned to me. "Thanks for letting me have that. I love the looks when I introduce myself." He looked back toward Ginger. "I was a trans woman before going through the process. I came out as my original male clone when I passed."

"Oh well, guess I can't up and order a male clone then, I guess I'll just be me. A me without this, I hope." She held up a shaky right hand.

"Oh, honey. Nerve damage?"

"ALS."

"That's a bad one. But never fear, we can make sure the new you is perfectly healthy."

He looked at me again. "Am I going to be getting any red flags or notices from the bosses?"

"Might get a red flag or two but this is fully sanctioned."

Janice entered my name in the computer. "Oh, this is a platinum package. There are no red flags for a platinum. In fact your uploads will be under a heightened security. Even the techs will be unable be in the room as the upload is being done."

He pointed toward the door. "You know the drill, Mister Turner. Go into the next room and lay on the table." He pointed at Ginger. "Now what name am I looking for, miss?"

I opened the door on the right as Ginger introduced herself.

It was several minutes before Janice entered to make sure I was situated on the table.

"You're all set. I'll come back when it's done."

"Gotcha," I said as the table slid into the hole. It was still uncomfortable.

He left by the same door he had entered, and I tried to relax for the process.

I was used to the process by now. We had to get an upload before every job we did on the road crews, so I'd been here quite a few times. I usually didn't get the same tech two times in a row though. There were a lot of techs that worked Gold Cross.

The door opened after the machine was done and Janice sat down behind the tech's desk as the table slid out of the machine.

"You're all done Mister Turner."

"Thanks." I sat up. "Everything all right?"

"Yes. Your lady friend is having a genetic sample taken. Our policy here is to be as neutral as possible, but I was happy to see your name cleared of the charges they brought against you. You should consider a defamation suit."

"This is the lawless lands. The Bolgeos and the Grollers run all of it. I doubt it would help to take a suit up against the company they run."

"You're probably right. Gold Cross is a multinational corporation. Sometimes I forget where I am." He chuckled. "If you were in Pennsylvania, you could win a large settlement."

"Instead I have to win a race. Or survive a race."

"I've seen the ads."

"I guess I'm not allowed to talk about it, but the ads are some fluffed up version of what I think we'll see out there. It ain't gonna be some arena with reinforced walls and purposefully weakened weapons. It's gonna be an ugly bitch."

"After seeing what you've experienced, I would tend to agree. Autoduelling was never my favorite thing, but I'll be watching your progress. Good luck, Mister Turner."

"It's never been my favorite thing either and even less so after participatin' in one of the arena bouts. That was ugly."

"I imagine so."

I shrugged and nodded toward the machine. "It got her this. That's what we're here for. Now all we have to do is get through this one race and she has it for life."

"Don't you wonder what you've signed up for when a platinum Gold Cross is the sign on?"

"Yeah, I do."

"As I said, Mister Turner, good luck."

"Probably gonna need all the luck we can get, Janice."

He nodded with a grim look.

"It was good to see you again," I said as I headed for the door. "But it's time to go see a lady about a car."

"Be careful out there."

"We'll do our best."

I stepped out into the hall to see Ginger waiting by the desk. Her face was a little paler than usual.

"You alright?" I asked as I stopped beside her. "Or is it just settin' in what we just did?"

"I just put a copy of me in a databank, Jake."

"I know. I've uploaded myself quite a few times so far. I updated it every time we went out on a job with the road crew. We'll need to come back periodically and update the file."

"How many times have you been here? That tech seemed to know you pretty well."

"He's been the tech who uploaded me a couple of times now. He's lucky he couldn't watch it." I chuckled.

"Are you sure no one can watch it?"

"Pretty sure, but who really knows?"

"They could watch things that are personal. Doesn't that worry you?"

"Not too much. They would run across some of the other stuff I've done and most of them would probably shy away from anything else."

"They might see you with me."

"That's not bad at all."

She giggled as we stepped out the door of Gold Cross. "What about that time I made you stop and go wash the mustard out of your beard before we could go any further?"

I laughed.

"I've missed that laugh, Jake Turner."

She slid in beside me as we walked down the stairs.

I missed that laugh too. They were few and far in between.

Chapter 27

"Ellen, do you know who the next sponsored team is yet?"

"Gavin, our next sponsored team is from just outside of Maynardville and they're called the Lutrell Legends. Brothers William and Robert Tackett are sponsored by the Fountain City Foundation after the Youngs' ordeal put them out of the running last month. Both of them are recovering, by the way, thanks to the intervention of the Blacktop Butchers in last month's Amateur Night. That was a particularly brutal arena duel with the deaths of four individuals."

"And it wasn't any typical arena battle either, Ellen. The mortality rate is substantially lower in the arena. But we can't really say the Butchers were wrong for doing what they did after both teams attacked the helpless Youngs, who were already out of the race. We all knew that Toxic was a vicious team but that was well beyond anything we expected out there."

"The Rabble Rousers weren't expected to join them either. Although being sponsored by the Vixens could have been a sure sign of what to expect."

"Well, Ellen, I guess cleaning up the streets is just another day's work for Jake Turner. After the trial brought forward the facts from his career as a Road Crew Guard. Judge Waits is well known for his opinions about excessive violence and still cleared Mister Turner of any wrongdoing which makes our Blacktop Butcher something entirely different."

"It also explains their actions during Amateur Night, Gavin. They came to the rescue of the Youngs instead of joining the assault. These actions align much better with something a little bit more … heroic."

"Heroic, indeed. I wonder what we'll have next Amateur Night to compare. It seems the Blacktop Butchers have set a high bar. That display of driving was epic and the ingenious use of the mine layer was quite devastating."

I grunted as I turned the radio off.

"Now we're heroes," Ginger said with a grin. "I like that so much better than the whole mass murderer thing. Is it too late, ma'am, to change our names to the Hometown Honey and the Killbilly?"

Charlie laughed. "Girl, you have to quit calling me ma'am."

"I told you, when you stop calling me girl I'd think about it."

"And yes, it's too late."

"Thank God," I said. "I don't think you'd be very happy bein' called a killbilly."

I chuckled as she looked at me with one eyebrow raised.

"He does have a sense of humor," Charlie said. "I was beginning to wonder."

"He drank a jar of shine." Ginger pointed toward the empty jar. "Sometimes the old Jake visits after he drinks enough. Would be a good time to do some live vids on the Clutch Stream."

I grunted.

"At least you can sit in the background looking ornery," she said. "That's what you're good at anyway. Now hush and look mean."

She triggered the screen with a remote. "Hey everyone! I'm Ginger Yates and this mean-looking lump is Jake Turner…"

Charlie watched from the side with a huge grin as she watched the icons begin to come alive. I was impressed with the volume of responses in such a short time. It was like they hovered and waited for someone to sign on. There would be one of these in the car with us when we ran the race so fans would be able to interact with us while it's going on.

My phone rang and I looked at it. It was Rob Flatford.

"I gotta take this," I said and stood up. "They're all here to see you, anyway."

"Come back when you're done," she said over her shoulder. "These are your fans, too."

"Nope they're not here to see the Hometown Honey. They wanna see you, killbilly." I walked out of sight of the camera before grinning. I looked back to see the reaction icons flooding across the screen. Comments began popping up so fast they couldn't all be read.

"Wow, people," Ginger said. "I can't even keep up. I'll do my best though…"

I answered the phone.

"Hey Rob."

"Jake."

"What can I do for you?"

"We need to talk, brother. I have some information you may want. Can you meet me outside of town?"

"Not sure if I can get away from the cameras that follow me around all the time, but I'll try."

"Don't worry about it. Meet me at the Dine and Dash out on I-40. Bill owes me a favor, and he's got top of the line jammers."

"I can do that. Give me a time."

"I'll be there as quick as you can get there."

"I'll head out now."

"You'll head where?" Charlie asked as she stepped into the kitchenette.

"Gotta meet someone at the Dine and Dash."

"You're not driving after drinking a whole jar of Larry's moonshine."

"I've done worse."

"Nevertheless, I'll drive."

I sighed. "All right. Need to ditch the cameras if possible."

"No worries. We learned ways around them years ago. It was hard to keep our identities secret when we were the Hoods, but we found ways."

It was close to an hour later when I walked into Wild Bill's Dine and Dash. It was on the site where a furniture store used to be. The huge sign with a squirrel still stood watch over the place but the furniture store was long gone. Wild Bill's was a pit stop and safe haven for anyone driving the roads. I was always glad to see the big brown squirrel as I entered the gates into Knoxville after any of the jobs we did out on I-40. Camera drones could be seen out near the gates but there were none that could get too close. The jammers would knock them out of the sky. Most of the time, the jammers were on and the Dine and Dash was neutral territory for anyone who came inside.

Occasionally there would be an event where the jammers shut down and the cameras were welcomed, like the wake they had done for Annabelle Axe and Fiona Fire after their demise. I wasn't even sure how I would be welcomed after that, but I wasn't interrupted on my way to the stairs that led to the upper floor. Charlie motioned toward the bar and headed in that direction.

At the top of the stairs there was a large platform with slightly fancier tables looking over the floor below. A large man in a suit held up a hand to stop me.

His eyes dropped to my jeans and flannel shirt.

I shrugged. "I'm expected."

His eyes narrowed and he typed something into his tablet. His surprise at the response was obvious.

"First door to the right and up the stairs."

At the top of the short stairway was a room with a large table in the middle, probably for high stakes card games. There was a single occupant.

"How the hell are ya, Jake?" Rob asked.

Chapter 28

I handed Charlie the paper Rob had given me as we settled back into the seats of the car.

"Jesus, Jake. Is this real?"

"You know the business better than I do. Would they do that?"

She let out a long breath. "Son of a… yes, they would. Ratings are tanking and they want a bloodbath like they had when they started autoduelling in the first place."

The paper she held was a copy of what TTA had sent out through every back channel they had access to.

"It's a bounty on every driver and gunner participating in the Dead Man's Run, and 'theoretical' expected route." I said. "And it's at least ten months ahead of the race."

"They'll be coming from all over to get their shot at it." Charlie laid the paper on the console between us. "Jake, I didn't know they would do something like this. We've got to pull out of it. This is a death sentence."

"Can't break that contract or this has all been for nothin'. Can't have that."

"They're restricting you to an arena level vehicle and they have assured that there will be combat from Knoxville, all the way to Memphis."

"Yep. It does reinforce what I was sayin' about what sort of car to build. We need armor and speed. They don't make a car that holds enough ammo to shoot everything between here and there."

"Did you not hear what I said? They'll be trying to kill you all, not just take out cars. You saw the line in the message where it had to be on screen? There's no upside to this."

"Can you give her a Gold Cross package?"

"I can barely afford mine," she said.

"Then this is the way."

"But—"

"Probably shouldn't tell her but I'd burn the world to ash for that woman. If I have to burn this little section to make sure she gets that package, I reckon I will."

"There'll be hundreds of raiders, rapists, and killers lined up from Knoxville to Memphis, Jake. And they don't have rules like the arena."

"Reckon that's what you call a target rich environment, ma'am," I said. "And rules? There ain't never been any rules out there. You been in this business long enough to know they'll change the rules anytime they want. But I saw that contract, just like you. If they break anything they put in that contract, we're free and clear."

"They don't have to break it. They've stacked the deck."

"I reckon they're not the only ones who can stack a deck, ma'am."

"What did you do?"

"When we leave these walls, there are no rules. For them or us. The only thing we have to do is succeed or die trying."

"The build is limited for the cars. They stacked the deck."

"We build for speed and durability. Jackie has somethin' cookin' with an old Vanguard she's havin' brought in from her yard. And Rob is grabbin' some salvage for me from down on I-75."

"Salvage?"

"Power plant and drives from a big rig."

"You've been researching. The power plant doesn't figure into the division rules."

"We get to start with a vehicle and a power plant. Reckon we'll start with somethin' that has natural armor to begin with and a plant that'll make her into a rocket on wheels."

"Alright, so what then?"

"We load that bitch with armor and blast through anything they put in front of us. If they can't catch us, they can't kill us."

"What's to keep them from following?"

"I expect they'll follow. We just have to stay ahead of 'em."

"That worries me." She glanced toward me.

"The biggest worry I have is gettin' the other winners on the same page," I said. "The whole 'runnin' in a pack' thing was unexpected. But if we're all on the same page, it'll help everyone get through it. The scoring system is fracked up, though. It's still a competition and 'packs' don't win this thing. The team with the most points wins. It's designed for treachery."

"Of course it is." She sighed. "I just don't see how anyone survives this. How does anyone even live out there?"

"There are good people out there and what this race is doin' is gonna endanger them. It'll attract some of the worst. But there are others out there that may be on the wrong side of the law that aren't like them. The ones comin' in will learn right quick what their boundaries are."

"You mean men like Flatford?"

"Yep."

"That still doesn't make me see how any of you will survive."

"We may not. But she'll survive with that Gold Cross."

"And you will."

"My clone will."

"Holy hell, you're doin' this and you're a Believer?"

"I was raised around Believers. I don't necessarily believe. I don't know what to believe. So far, I haven't had to find out."

"How the hell did Larry raise a Believer?"

"I'm not. Hell, Pop hates Believers."

"He should. Especially after what they did."

"What?"

"He didn't tell you about Lizzie?"

"She died in an accident."

"That was most certainly not an accident. It was a terrorist act by radical Believers. They bombed Gold Cross while she was inside. We lost her and her upload all at once." She paused. "I guess that wasn't for me to tell you, but you need to know it. It's why my dad never spoke to Larry again. Dad always swore he should have been there to protect Lizzie. After Dad retired, I tried to get Larry to do another update, but he said he wasn't interested in living on without her."

"I never knew any of that."

"He doesn't talk about it much. It's painful. He was supposed to go with her, but he had a load of whiskey that needed delivered. He promised to go later that week. After the way Dad treated him, I was surprised he called me."

"He did that for me. I was looking for a way to help Ginger."

"I'm still surprised. My dad used him for years to make money and threw him away when Larry needed him. He was a wreck for years, but he kept going for you. There's no denying that."

"He's always been there for me. I did him wrong when I ran off. I do regret that."

"This." she raised the note from the console. "This is going to tear him up. He always hated the killing. He refused to do it in the arena. He hated that you had to kill in your first autoduel."

"Some people need killin', ma'am."

"God, would you stop with the ma'am? Makes me feel like I'm in my sixties or something."

I chuckled.

"Oh, son of a bitch, I am in my sixties! You can stop reminding me any time, though."

160 | P a g e

Chapter 29

"What have I done, Charlie?" Pop asked. I'd never heard that sort of despair in his voice before. Even when he lost Gran, he hid it from me.

"You gave them a chance."

"At what cost?"

"What do you think he would have done otherwise? What would you have done for Lizzie?"

He was silent for a moment. "Damn it, Charlie."

"I know, Lar. You would have done anything it took. Hell, what you did do was more than my father ever did."

"What?"

"Don't act like we both don't know about that Believer cell. Everyone involved disappeared. I suspect if they dragged Norris Lake there'd be a lot of questions answered."

"I don't know what you're talkin' about," he said. "Nobody wants to drag that lake, anyway. Lot more than Believers at the bottom of it."

I hated being an eavesdropper, but I had learned more about my grandfather in a few moments than I had all of my life. I backed away from the door silently and reached out to shut the bathroom door with a light thud so they could hear it.

They were both sipping coffee as I entered the room. I chuckled as I walked to the kitchenette for my own cup.

"What are you laughin' at, boy?"

"Just remembering all the days I walked into the living room, and you'd be sittin' there drinking coffee." I shook my head. "Sorry I ran off on you."

"Sometimes you have to run off and go find yourself, kid. Sometimes you like what you find, sometimes you don't. But you always find somethin'."

"True enough. So what was that about Norris Lake?"

"We were just talkin' bout fishin'," he said.

"Yeah, there's some good spots down in the Chapel. Reckon Jackie was telling me about this old quarry down near end of Leadmine Bend. Deep water. Big catfish down there, I mean big enough to swallow a man whole. Reckon if they dragged that lake, they wouldn't find much down there but catfish shit."

He laughed. "How much of that did you hear?"

"Enough. Pop, while I was out there finding myself, I found a whole lot of evil people and I can say for a certainty that some people need killin'. I reckon them fellers were some of them."

"They were."

"Then they're right where they ought to be. I've done my share of sending folks like that to Hell where they can join 'em. The reality of what's comin' is that there's gonna be a whole bunch more joining them soon. Now I'm gonna go do something that I never thought I'd be doing. I'm gonna go warn those boys from Maynardville what TTA has in store for us before they sign contracts."

"These days in autoduelling, it probably won't matter." Charlie stood up. "There's a death almost every Amateur Night and the pro circuit has death aplenty."

"Still have to try. Even if they continue, they might alter the builds they plan to be more defensive." I sipped my coffee. "Reckon I'll visit the twins as well. Everyone needs to know what's coming."

"I miss the days when it was a sport. We tried to take out cars, not people." Pop shook his head.

"Those days left with the Hoods," Charlie said. "It got dark afterwards in Knoxville and the surrounding areas. Frankly, none of what they did here has really surprised me. I hate it but I'm not surprised. We dropped Knoxville from our normal circuit a long time ago. We do the AADA Championships, but nothing else here."

"Never had much use for autoduelling until now," I said. "But this'll get the job done and she'll have a future."

"Speaking of Ginger, where is she?"

"Sleepin' in, I reckon. She got into the shine last night while she was on the Clutch Stream. Ended up in some sort of drinkin' game."

"Did you play?"

"Didn't really have to. I was drinkin' already. Reckon some of these fellers around here ain't able to hold their liquor. After everybody passed out, I shut down the Stream and got Gin tucked in."

"Then you crashed?" Charlie nodded.

"It was just twelve. I went to the bar. Crashed about two this mornin'."

"Jesus, Jake. How much did you drink?"

"Enough." I turned to Pop. "I was lookin' at some of the accessories we can put in the car and if you see Jackie today, tell her I want one of those Beer Fridges. I like my liquor cold, and ice is for amateurs."

"You plan to be drinking?" Charlie was aghast.

"You don't think I'm doin' this shit show sober, do you?" I asked as I opened the door and stepped out of the room into the hallway where the floating cameras waited.

"Is he serious?" I heard as the door closed.

I chuckled. I was half joking but the more I thought about it, the less joke there was. Enough alcohol could numb the hate I felt for what I had become. I could try to shift back toward the guy I used to be, but I was afraid that guy wouldn't get too far where we were going.

I could hate the man I had become all I wanted but I would need him out there. She would need him out there. When the time came for her to see that, I would be prepared for the repercussions. I couldn't see a future where we would be able to go back to what we once were. Not after she sees that. And so I drink until I'm numb, until it doesn't matter anymore.

"Seems to take more and more," I muttered.

One of the cameras swooped in closer.

"Piss off." I pushed it aside and entered the elevator. "You can take the next one."

I never made it a secret that I hated the cameras. That was why my rating remained low and Ginger's was skyrocketing. Everyone loved her, which was something I understood completely. Lately the Hometown Honey moniker seemed to have gained ground. So had the Killbilly, apparently. I didn't really care overmuch. It wasn't any worse than the I-75 Butcher which they called me before that.

My phone pinged and I shook my head. Probably another attempt by TTA to get me to release the footage Judge Wait had witnessed during my trial. They wanted to use it for advertising, guaranteeing an increase in my personal ratings. I raised it to find, sure enough, another in a long line of messages from TTA's affiliate television network, Titan Communications. TiCom had been after me for the footage since the trial.

I wasn't about to do that. They offered a lot of money but not enough to buy a Gold Cross for Ginger. It would be the only way I'd release that footage. It would be worth that to be able to just walk away from all of this nonsense.

Chapter 30

I stepped into the garage just as one of the brothers closed the hood on what looked like a vintage Galahad. He stopped as he turned and saw me

"Tazewell," he said with his head cocked to the side a fraction.

I nodded.

He sniffed and spit to his right. I could see his jaw bulged out a little where his chewing tobacco was.

"Whatcha want, Tazewell?"

"Just goin' round, meetin' the team."

"Team?"

"You haven't read the contract yet?"

"Bout to read it this evenin'."

"They have us runnin' all twelve teams as a pack. We all work together to get through the race."

"What the hell they do somethin' like that for?"

"That's why I'm here. I wanted to give you and your brother a heads up on what they're doin' before you go and sign."

"Tazewell."

The voice that came from the right side of the car was almost identical, as was the guy that stepped around the open door of the Galahad. Both had long reddish brown hair and sported the same braided goatee. The only difference was the size of the second brother. He was an identical copy, only smaller. He was a good six inches shorter than his brother.

"Just as well you're both here," I said and pulled the paper from my pocket. "This is somethin' you fellas might want to look at."

The smaller of the two stepped forward and took the paper.

"Tazewell."

Another identical voice came from the door to the office as it opened. This one was another carbon copy, only he was huge.

The smallest one chuckled. "That one always gets 'em."

"Clones? Ain't that illegal?"

"Nah we're bona fide. Momma was nature's own cloning factory," The smallest brother said."

"Triplets?" I asked. "Or is there another one of you about to pop up?"

"Only three," he said. "I'm Robert." He pointed at the middle one. "This is my brother, William and my other brother William."

I let out a long breath. "It's gonna be like that, huh?"

Robert laughed. "Not as bad as all that. He's William Joseph and he's Joseph William. Bobby, Billy, and Joe. He's the runt of the litter."

He looked down at the paper. "Son o' ma bitch! Take a look at this, Billy."

After the brothers read the message, the three of them stood there for a moment.

"I don't reckon it changes everything too much," Bobby said. "We knew it was gonna be rough when they announced our route was going to be public two months ahead of the race, but this is some grade A bullshit right here."

"At least the bounty is just on you two dipshits," Joe, the largest of the three said.

"We're the ones what got the Gold Crosses. They couldn't rightly do it to the mechanic."

Bobby handed me the letter. "Is that a message to Rob Flatford? Is he gonna be after us?"

There was a genuine tone of worry in his voice.

"Rob was a little pissed when he got this and called me. He's not interested in claiming that bounty. But you and I both know there are hundreds of others that would love to. Our sponsors want us to die on screen. I just felt you fellas should know before you sign up for it."

"So what's in it for you, Tazewell? There ain't much more than hate between Tazewell and Maynardville?"

"I don't reckon I hate anyone in Maynardville. A little upset with the Tollivers after they shot at me, but I don't really hate 'em."

"Tollivers shoot at everybody." Bobby drew a cigar from his pocket and licked it. "They're aim is shit, so they're mostly harmless."

"Figured as much, so I didn't kill any of 'em."

He chuckled.

"As far as what's in it for me? I reckon a team workin' together has a better chance of getting' to the other side. I've been out there when there wasn't a whole bunch of raiders and there's been a lot of deaths. With the amount that this is gonna bring in, I would really think about the builds we use."

"Like what?" Will, the giant mechanic, asked. "What kind of guns does the I-75 Butcher recommend?"

I grunted. "Guess everybody's gonna be bringin' that up. What I'm suggestin' is to get a well armored frame and a big power plant. Then armor it some more. And after that, armor it some more."

"Weapons?"

"I doubt we can carry enough ammo to kill what they're gonna throw at us. But I never go unarmed. We have a Vanguard with a power plant and the drivetrain out of a semi. Gonna have a buffalo gun in a turret and all the ammo I can haul. Everything else goes into armor and suspension. I'd love some Vulcans, but they eat up ammo too fast. Raiders are typically in stock vehicles, but they don't have the restrictions on weapons we'll have as we leave the gate. Our weapons are rated for arena matches. That's why I want armor."

"A power plant from a semi?" Will laughed. "How you gonna keep it on the ground?"

"Enough armor to keep it on the ground and Ginger at the wheel."

Bobby chuckled. "I saw some of those races they showed after you two won. Girl can drive almost as good as me."

"I really hope you're right. I know how well she drives. If you're better, it's just a bonus. If you're talkin' shit, that's okay too. You won Amateur Night and that says plenty."

"And you've either done us a solid or set us up to go out there with hardly any weapons. So we have to decide if you're talkin' shit too."

"True enough," I said. "I'll leave you to it."

"One thing first?" Billy asked.

"Yup."

"Is it true you were the guy that took out the Crossbones over in Cookeville?"

"It is."

"I know a guy that was held there, and he tells one hell of a story."

"You know how things get blown out of proportion."

"Yeah. I thought it was a little out there. No way that story could be true."

"Probably not."

I turned and walked back out of the garage. I wished that story would go away and take the memory of it along with it. It was not my best moment. That was the night that changed me forever.

Sometimes I think it would have been better to have died with the rest of the crew. I wouldn't remember those days of agony … and the things I did afterwards.

Chapter 31

"Uncle Albert's sure to have your every desire," said a cute blonde in a tiny bikini top and urban camouflage pants as she stepped into view on the screen. She carried a light machine gun, holding it in both hands with two belts of ammo that she wore crisscrossed over her chest.

"Don't settle for those imitation brand names. Uncle Al's guarantees the largest selection from coast to coast!"

Weapons systems flashed across the screen. Autocannons, flame throwers, machine guns, mines, lasers, and rocket launchers faded in and out of view. "If it's in stock, we got it!" she yelled, bouncing to show off her other accessories. "Uncle Albert gives you the weapons, gadgets, and accessories you need! But don't take my word for it!"

The picture changed to a pair of autoduellists standing in front of a well-used Smokin' Joe. "Uncle Albert has saved our tailpipes more times than I can count. Without his overnight delivery and dirt cheap prices, there's no way we could ever keep up with the corporate teams no matter how much of a socket-brained slushbox they are."

"Thanks, Uncle Albert," the gunner said, shooting his hand cannon into the sky.

The cute blonde reappeared with a mini rocket resting in her lap.

"Guaranteed, you won't find prices lower than ours for your autoduelling needs."

I chuckled as the commercial faded to black. Uncle Al's was bombarding the air waves as the Dead Man's Run got closer and closer.

"With that, I'm out." Ginger tapped her tablet and closed it down.

"What?" I asked as I shut off the screen on the wall.

"You missed someone asking for access to make personal vids with me."

"TTA? They keep askin' for access to those court vids for advertising."

"No. Just some adult only channel."

"Hmph."

"I swear, some people are pigs." She closed her tablet. "It's not even just men. Some of the things a few of these women want to do is insane."

"Men are mean, but women are vicious." I was lost in a memory for a short moment. "They'll hurt someone a lot more than the men will."

"What?"

"I read about the Apache tribes in the old west." I hadn't been thinking about them, but it was still the truth. "They loved to torture anyone they caught."

"Oh."

"Cherokee were a little more civilized," I said.

"Were they? Or are you a little biased?"

"Maybe. I'm part Cherokee. But the Apache were some right mean bastards."

"Did you see the Tacketts signed the contract?" she asked.

"Figured they still planned on it. Didn't seem to worry them as much after I told them Rob wasn't comin' after us."

"Is Flatford that dangerous?"

"And then some."

"Well I'm glad he's your friend, then. That's one less crazy out there lined up to kill us."

"He's not crazy," I said. "He's ruthless if you're an enemy. But he'll do anything for his people. Lot to be admired in the man."

"I didn't mean he was crazy. Just looking ahead at what they're doing. It's going to be a hell of a drive to get through them."

"It will. We'll have a thirty mile or so buffer from the gates of Knoxville, if things stay as they are, but I'd say Crossville is gonna be a beast."

"If they stay as they are?"

"TTA is just as likely to pull that buffer as leave it."

She sighed and leaned back in the chair. "Speaking of Flatford, the power plant arrived today. I'm not sure where he got it, but it has some scorch marks on it. Jackie said it won't hurt the performance any."

"It came out of a wrecked semi down on I-75." I picked up the jar on the end table and took a drink. "I told him about it a couple weeks ago. He said he'd pick it up and look it over."

"Was that where the attack happened?"

"Yup."

"And TTA just let you have it?" she asked.

"I didn't ask 'em."

"How come no one else already got it?"

"No one knew about it but TTA and me."

"What about the crew?"

"They only remember up to their last upload. That's why you'll wanna upload any chance you get to keep it as current as you can."

She was silent for a moment. "Jake, you don't have to do this. Just walk away. You got me to where I needed. I have a Gold Cross, now."

"That's not how this works," I said. "I walked away before and turned myself into a monster. I've done things that you can't even imagine." I stood up with the jar in my hand and took a drink. "Pop says life is a series of crucibles. You go in one person and come out the other side someone different. There'll be many crucibles along the way and each of 'em will change you. I failed you in the first of those. I'm still evaluating whether the next was a failure or a success. It certainly prepared me for the one coming."

"Jake…" she stood and reached out.

I shook my head and turned away. "You haven't seen it yet. When you do…"

I shook my head again and walked out of the suite. I wasn't the same man she had known before, and I figured she'd see that soon enough. It was only a few months away.

There had been three other Amateur Nights since I talked to the Tacketts. I warned every one of them as soon as they finished their event so they would have an accurate idea of what awaited us out there. Every one of them still signed up for the Dead Man's Run, but I also noticed a change in the builds of several. The Tacketts were focusing on armor, but I wasn't even sure there was enough armor to soak up what was going to by flying at us.

Crossville was always a rough place but now it was crawling with roving gangs that were making it hard on the locals. Cookeville was seeing an influx of the same sort of people.

"Penny for your thoughts," Pop leaned on the wall beside the door to my suite. "You look troubled."

"Reckon I'll look troubled for a while, Pop." I opened the door and let him precede me into the room. "Worried about Max and his family out in Cookeville."

"Max?"

"He was the one that found me after that thing in Cookeville. Took me in and patched what he could til the company got someone out there to get me. He's good people and he doesn't deserve the shit storm that's descended on the area."

"There's a lot of folks that don't deserve this," he said. "You hear about the speedway?"

"The speedway?"

"Yeah, the old Nashville Speedway. There's a group that's moved in there. They're cannibals."

"Cannibals?"

"Yep. It's not like that's the only thing they eat but they're claimin' they plan to catch every one of the racers and, well, they plan to do cannibal things."

"Frack me, this just gets better and better. Cannibals? Who the frack does that?"

"Hell, they got a bunch of these guys to take up residence in Memphis in that great big pyramid. They got two levels of crime there. You get fined or you get thrown into the pyramid. You make it out the other side, I reckon they figure you paid your debt to society."

"I'm guessin' there ain't many that get out the other side."

"You'd be guessin' right." He sat down in the chair across from the couch. "Reckon it ain't a new thing. Been there for years."

"So now we don't just die, we get to be lunch for a bunch of deviants. I ever tell you I hate this shit?"

"It used to be a little more civilized. I spent four and a half years on the circuit, and I didn't have to kill anyone. Came pretty close a few times but I managed to leave the arena without fatalities. It was a sport. Have I killed a few? Yes. Out in the badlands I may have had to do that but not in the arena. I wasn't cryin' any tears up on Clinch Mountain. The arena has gotten more and more deadly."

"Then they come up with this shit show," I said.

There was a knock and Charlie entered the suite.

I waved as I stood. "Gonna hit the sack. Gotta go meet the newest pair in the mornin' before they go sign up."

"Night, kid."

I stepped into the bedroom and let the door close behind me most of the way.

"I just fed the only thing left of her into this meat grinder."

"You know he had to do something for her. What would you have done for Lizzie?"

"Hell I'd have done anything if it would bring her back."

"He said he would burn the world for that girl. What you gave him is a way to save her. You think he wouldn't have seen something about this race if you hadn't told him?"

"He hates autoduelling."

"Look at what it's become. I hate it too. All we can do is give them every advantage we can. I've been in contact with his friend, Flatford. Come with me, I have something to show you."

Chapter 32

"One more month to go, ladies and gentlemen! The last Amateur Night has come to an end with the victory of Primal Rage! The countdown to the event of the century begins here and now!" Gavin Grey yelled.

"That's right, Gavin!" his co-host, Ellen Mayor, answered. "We have one hell of a group of drivers and gunners. We have the Twin Terrors, Axel and Terry Bunch. Siblings with a penchant for violence, as we saw in the first match."

"Next, we have the Blacktop Butchers, Ginger Yates, driver extraordinaire. She's partnered with the I-75 Butcher, himself, Jake Turner," Gavin said. "Social media has been calling them the Hometown Honey and the Killbilly after the sensational events around their joining of the roster."

"They are followed by the Lutrell Legends, triplets William, Joseph, and Robert Tackett. Two of the brothers will be in the car and the other is their mechanic who will fly ahead to the stopping point of the first leg of the Dead Man's Run.

"Next up, Ellen, is the team out of Maryville sponsored by Telbot Industries after they replaced the Maryville Madmen who were removed from the competition early in the year. Damage, Inc. put on a great show as they tore through the other cars in their custom Bombardier. Driver David Munseizer and gunner Oscar Polk are going to be characters to watch in my opinion."

I tuned out the announcers on the TV hanging above the bar. I sat in one of the furthest back booths where no one could really see me clearly. Ginger was up doing another live Clutch Feed and I wasn't in the mood.

Sure enough, they'd removed the thirty mile buffer from the walls of Knoxville. As soon as we left the walls we would be under attack. The only advantage we had was the order to keep the highway clear. Under no circumstance were there any roadblocks allowed on our stretch of interstate. Our course was preset, and it was called a race for a reason. The camera delay was about the only other thing that would be going for us. The broadcast would be happening right at two hours after the live events so the network could do their thing and prep the announcers for what they would say.

"Drinkin' alone, Tazewell?"

"Didn't much wanna talk to any of this crowd," I grunted as Robert Tackett sat down at the booth.

"Can't rightly blame you." He sipped his beer. "The boys and me decided you were right and set the ole Galahad up for speed. I saw you over here and figured I'd run some ideas by you."

"A guy from Tazewell?"

"Nobody's perfect, except maybe me."

I chuckled.

"You did us a solid when you warned us bout that bounty and some of the others agreed. We figured you might know a little bout what's out there after workin' the road crews. Figured it'd be a good time to sit down and make a plan."

"I figure we run together and guard each other's flanks. That is if they listened about buildin' for speed. Reckon I'll talk to Southard and Bolder tomorrow."

"Most of us took your advice," he said. "You may be from Tazewell but even a broke clock is right twice a day. I talked to those two a little while ago, right after the event. They're onboard."

"Good."

"I say most 'cause Thunder Road and the Sons of Liberty both just blew it off. I saw their builds. They got a lot of guns but no extra speed. Question is, if we run as a pack, what happens with them?"

"Do we risk ten teams to protect two who wouldn't listen?"

"I think that's somethin' that needs to be asked," he said. "Don't you?"

"Unfortunately, I agree. I think I know the answer already."

"That's good too, cause I already asked everybody. We can't hang back for 'em."

"I kinda figured that would be the answer," I said.

"So now I got a question for you, Tazewell. I looked at your build, too. With that damn semi's drive motors and power plant, you can leave every one of us in the dirt. Why wouldn't you?"

"Mutual defense." I took a long drink from the bottle. "To be blunt, the more cars around us, the more armor there is between her and a bullet."

"And you."

"True enough."

"Alright then. That's a valid answer, Tazewell, and an honest one." He took another drink from his beer. "I can see where them havin' to shoot through you to get to me is a positive."

I held my bottle out and he tapped the beer bottle to it. "Mutual defense."

"Mutual defense." He nodded and took a drink. "Careful, now, Tazewell. I might even get to like you a little."

"We couldn't have that, now, could we?"

"Hell no."

"So did you tell the Sons of Liberty and Thunder Road that we can't hang back, or do I need to? They still have a month to get their speed up."

"I told 'em. They called me a runt and a coward. Not both at the same time, though or it might have hurt my feeling"

"Your feeling? You only got one?"

"Damn right. And they almost hurt it. Luckily, the Sons of Liberty just called me a runt. Thunder Road called me a coward, I think they actually meant all of us so it spread the hurt around. Can you feel it too? Just checkin', cause if it didn't spread just a little, I'd have to feel all of it, and I might do somethin' drastic."

"Don't worry bout it," I said with a grin. "I'm feelin' it too. Thing is, I got a few more feelings to spread that hurt on so it's not quite as strong."

"Oh thank God. That Muncey fella's a little scary. Looks like a damn Bigfoot."

"Maybe you should introduce him to Joe."

"Now that'd be somethin', wouldn't it? Little Joe and the Bigfoot."

I chuckled.

"I gotta get out of here." He stood and held his mostly empty bottle out. "Gotta talk to a fella bout some bullets for the buffalo gun."

"Good choice in weapons."

"Figured I'd be able to scavenge yours if you get killed."

"True enough."

"That didn't even get a reaction? Damn it, man."

I grinned.

He shook his head. "Catch ya later, then. One more month and we're all probably gonna be on our way to get downloaded into frackin' clones anyway." He held his fingers up as quotations "At least they aren't allowed to block the roads."

"I know. Right? Villains do villain shit."

He laughed. "I'm gonna use that one."

I took another long drink from the bottle. I was almost there. I almost didn't hate myself. Maybe he was right. Maybe we would all be clones in a couple months and start new. I wondered if my clone would hate himself, too.

Chapter 33

"Is everyone ready for race day?" Gavin Grey's voice resounded from the massive speakers just inside the gates.

I could hear the roar of the crowds even inside our Vanguard.

"Then how about we start this thing! Welcome all to the Dead Man's Run!"

The crowd roared again.

I tuned the crowd and announcer out and placed the helmet over my head. A mystery sponsor had provided us with a new sensor suite and drone package much like the one in Pop's Conestoga.

"First, we have the Twin Terrors, Axel and Terry Bunch, in their modified Dragon from Indra Motors. It looks a little light on weaponry though."

"I seem to be seeing a pattern here Gavin," Ellen Mayor said. "Most of our vehicles today seem to be armor heavy and weapon light."

"I suppose we'll see if these brave souls have chosen a wise strategy or not, Ellen."

"As I look out across the distance of interstate, Gavin, I feel like it might have been a good choice. I've never seen so many vehicles just waiting for our steadfast car warriors."

"I can't help but agree, Ellen. In the second spot we have the Blacktop Butchers in their heavily armored Vanguard II. The single weapon on that turret may be a heavy hitter but it is still a single weapon. From what I can see, that armor is going to be a beast though. It's going to hinder their speed though."

"It might at that, Gavin. Although I have heard rumors of oversized power plants and drives from several of the teams."

"Let's hope it's true, Ellen, or this may be a short race."

"Next we have the Lutrell Legends in a heavily armored Galahad," she said. "I'm getting a definite pattern here."

My HUD flashed with a call from Pop. I tuned out the announcers as they introduced the other racers.

"Hey Pop, missed you this mornin' when we left."

"Sorry kid, had to ship out early to catch my ride." The noise in the background was loud.

"What are you ridin' in?"

"Chopper's noisy as hell."

"We're about to hit the gates in about ten minutes. Tell Jackie we're about to see what this drive will do."

He nodded. "Will do. You be careful, kid. Run the wheels off that damn Vanguard."

"Yes, Sir."

"I gotta go, kid. But always remember I love ya."

"Love you too, Pop."

I hung up but I couldn't shake the feeling something seemed off.

"That didn't sound like a chopper to me."

"What?" Ginger asked.

"Nothin'. You ready to race?"

"Always ready to race."

I reached over and opened the fridge to remove a jar.

"Drinking, already? It's seven o'clock."

"Just gettin' an early start. You see what that camera showed when she talked about outside?"

"You have a point. Pass me the jar."

She took a small drink and passed it back. "Damn that burns."

I took a long swig and put it back in the fridge. "Yep."

"You're right though. It is better cold."

"Here we go." The lights beside the gate turned orange and the massive gates swung outward. I rested my head against the headrest. I remembered the Hammer we were in, and this one had a hell of a lot more power.

The light turned green.

I remember stories when I was young about placing a hundred-dollar bill on the dash with tape and if the passenger could grab it in a certain amount of time, they could have it. That's the kind of acceleration the Vanguard had. I was pinned to my seat with my hands grasping the controls for the Buffalo gun.

I grinned and watched my HUD.

I was pretty sure we were expected to come out the gate accelerating but I'm pretty sure no one expected us to exit the gate already up to eighty miles per hour and gaining speed at an impressive rate. At ninety-five the acceleration eased off. We hadn't reached our top speed or even gotten close to it, but we couldn't run off and leave the others.

"Damnit, man! I thought you were gonna run off there for a minute," Bobby Tackett said.

"It's a damned rocket," Ginger said.

"Alright, guys, let's pull in tight," I said. "It's about to get messy."

I was watching the HUD and we'd ripped past at least thirty cars poised on the side of the interstate waiting for us, but they were realizing our speed and getting off the line a lot quicker ahead of us so they could intercept.

The bad part was watching my HUD as those thirty unloaded on the pair that hadn't built their cars for speed.

Thunder Road didn't make it a half of a mile before smoke bellowed out of burst windows.

"Shit," I muttered.

"Oh my God!"

"Don't think about it. Nothin' we can do for 'em."

"That's what they wanted isn't it? TTA wanted that for all of us?"

"They still do. Watch out, three o'clock."

"I see them."

Bullets peppered the Vanguard, and she swerved right, clipping the car full of gun waving idiots. It was hardly more than a rail buggy and the front collapsed when the armored van hit.

"Oh Jesus," she said as the front dropped and the rear of the car rose to the sky.

Bodies rained down on the highway. "Don't even look at 'em. They were here for the specific reason of killing us."

More of the buggies were closing with the others. They didn't have any armor, so they were the fastest of the pursuit cars.

Billy Tackett dropped the buffalo gun to point right into the cab of a truck. The heavy round transformed the driver to a red mist and the truck swayed back and forth a few times before heading to the left, right into the path of another pickup. Fire erupted from the other truck as it slammed into the side of the first and ruptured a battery cell.

"Don't waste ammo on these unarmored guys," I said. "Just run over their asses. We got a couple of heavies incoming, shoot those frackers."

More and more vehicles were coming in from the side and I practiced what I preached as I sent three shots through the side of a RAW Morningstar. It had a bit of armor, but my third shot was a depleted uranium round, and it did something ugly inside the car. Fire filled the interior, and it swerved hard toward us.

Ginger punched the accelerator, and we jumped forward, barely missing the incoming wreck. Then we dropped back into formation.

My HUD showed the Sons of Liberty as they took a rocket from a handheld launcher.

"Damn," I muttered.

"I tried to warn them," Bobby said.

"All you can do is try," Jon Bolder of Primal Rage responded. "They had the same warning we all did."

I looked ahead at the lines of cars on the sides of the interstate as they began moving.

"This is gonna get ugly," I said.

Chapter 34

"Gavin, I'm not sure if I've ever seen anything like this before! Less than a mile in and two teams are down!"

"I guess that answers the question about the builds. Speed and armor seem to be a team's best friend today in the Dead Man's Run."

"Speaking of speed, Gavin, I have never seen a Vanguard move like that and I've seen a few of them in action. I think the rumors of power plant enhancement just might be true."

"They slowed down to stay with the pack. Someone's been looking at that line of cars ahead of them with the sole purpose of ending this leg of the race before it ever gets started. That's a smart move for the Butchers."

"Diamond formation," I said as I used my HUD to show them my suggestion.

"Looks good to me," David Munseizer answered. "Smaller gunner arc."

"That's the idea," I said. "We'll take the point. Heaviest armor."

"No complaints here." Bobby laughed. "Guy in the front gets shot at more."

I grinned as he settled into the rear of the diamond. "At this speed, the back'll probably get shot at more."

"Son o' ma bitch!"

"Comin' in on both sides," I said. "Here we go. Sure miss those twin Vulcans on Charlene."

Shots impacted our side armor.

I swung the buffalo gun to the right and put a shot right into the driver side door of an AI Piranha that erupted in fire.

"Oops," I said. "That was a DU round."

My HUD was starting to look like a Christmas tree with all of the lights and they were closing in around us.

I designated eight targets and sent them to the other gunners. Then I zeroed in on mine, putting three shots into the front tire of a scratched-up Indra DT. The front dropped and the car couldn't compensate. It pulled inward and the DT started rolling. We shot ahead of the closing group on the right as the rolling wreck took out two more incoming cars.

Most of the gunners took the shots at the designated targets with similar results. It left the whole interstate behind us blocked by the pileup. It took the great majority of the chase vehicles out of the running.

"Good call, Tazewell," Bobby said. "You some kinda idiot savant of destruction?"

"You got the first part right," Ginger said.

Unfortunately, the roads were still lined with cars joining the chase. Five miles and they were still lining the roads. Worse, some of them were figuring out that we were running faster than they expected and coming onto the highway in front of us.

"What? Leave them behind? That's a dick move!"

"Who the hell are you talkin' to?" I asked.

"Clutch stream…" She swerved to the right as we caught up to one of the cars that had gotten on the road ahead of us.

She tapped the back of what my HUD identified as a Mako just before it could fire its turret. It fired just over our head with a gout of napalm a second before it completely left the ground and began spinning in the air.

"Jesus!" yelled Axel Bunch of the Twin Terrors as the Mako, still rolling in the air, passed over them only inches away.

It clipped the rear spoiler before hitting the pavement. The impact must have ruptured the tank as the inside of the Mako became a furnace.

"Good tap!" Larry Southard cheered.

I glanced at the Clutch feed that was installed at both of our stations. There was a bunch of coin icons and green dollar icons rolling across the screen. I didn't have a clue what they were for, but I was too busy to worry about that.

Something thumped beside me, and I cursed. Tracking the fire with my HUD, I put a depleted Uranium round into a guy about a hundred yards off of the road.

"What the hell, Tazewell. Thought we were savin' ammo for cars."

I sent an image with my helmet.

"Oh hell no! He shot the beer fridge?"

I put my hand on the side of the fridge. "Still workin'. I'm good."

The dots on my HUD kept growing so I launched the drones to get better coverage.

"Obsidian Corporation did us a solid with this sensor package," I said as the drones reached their altitude.

"See what social media will do?" Ginger responded.

"I still hate it."

"There's a couple of Clutch Bunnies on here that want to have your babies."

I didn't even have an answer for that. She was right. There were two women arguing on the feed about which got to go first.

"Frack," I muttered.

The drones picked up a Hammer up ahead that was dropping mines so I marked each of them on the HUD and sent it to the others, marking a route for each of us so we wouldn't hit them.

"Dude, your sensor suite is off the chain!" Samantha Sinn of the Painted Ladies yelled.

The mines were coming up fast and we shot through the gaps. Explosions rocked the highway behind us as the pursuing cars hit the mines.

The minelayer was in range, and I put three shots into the power plant. The car slowed a great deal, and we shot past it.

"Thanks for the help, whoever you are!" Bobby Tackett laughed.

"Incoming!" I yelled as my sensors picked up the rocket. It had been fired by a handheld launcher.

It impacted the armored glass of the Twin Terrors' Dragon and exploded inside the car.

I grimaced as Axel and Terry Bunch were consumed in the inferno and their Dragon shot off to the right to impact an incoming Bombardier. The Dragon and the Bombardier were both big vehicles but a collision at those speeds sent them careening off of the highway into a deep ditch.

"Shit!"

"That was an anti-tank rocket!" Bobby sounded shaken.

I understood. One shot and we were down another team. There wasn't much doubt if they were dead. I was pretty sure no one could live through that inferno.

"Oh hell!" I scowled. "That don't look good at all."

Coming in from the ramp in Harriman was something huge.

"It's got Vulcans on top of it!" Bobby shouted as I shared the image.

"Frack me!" Larry Southard of Primal Rage added.

My phone rang.

An image of Rob Flatford was grinning at me from the screen.

"Now don't you folks get all worried, now. We decided to join the party." He panned the phone around to point at a familiar form in a large gunner station.

I connected the rest of the pack to the call.

"Why is that guy dressed like Jeremy Hood?" Jon Bolder asked.

"Let me introduce you, friends, to one of the greatest gunners ever to grace an Arena. Jeremy has decided to join us for the festivities! And our lovely driver is none other than Kelly Hood, herself!"

As the semi left the ramp, the top of it erupted in fire as two dual Vulcans opened fire on the cars that were set to join in the attack.

Rob giggled. "Oh, it looks like we've started the party."

His southern drawl was unmistakable. "Just tuck right here, alongside, my little ducklings! For this little stretch of road you have yourselves a linebacker!"

196 | P a g e

Chapter 35

"Ladies and gentlemen, of all the things I expected from this race, this is not one of them! Remember, those of you at home, we are two hours behind the actions that took place in this next segment! I almost couldn't contain myself when it happened and went live."

"I know, Gavin," Ellen said. "How could you not want to run with the reappearance of the Hoods after their retirement?"

"That's right, Ellen. Sponsors of our race teams are allowed to drop supplies and money at any given time to the racers, but this might be the most novel approach I have ever seen. Let's go straight to the call from this sponsor."

"Hello America," Rob said with his southern drawl. "I am Robert Flatford of Bobby Ray Flatford Industries, named after my great grandfather. We chose to sponsor several of these teams, today."

There was a large burst of gunfire and Rob giggled.

"We decided to donate several hundred thousand 20-millimeter rounds to our intrepid friends."

More gunfire filled the air.

"Unfortunately none of our friends could use this particular caliber so I decided we should disperse these for them. Along with me is my friend, Jeremy Hood, who is more than happy to deliver this donation for me. Driving our donation dispersal unit is none other than the beautiful and talented Kelly Hood."

"I knew that wasn't a chopper," I muttered.

"What was that?" Rob asked.

"Nothin'."

"It is my understanding that there are a wide array of miscreants lined up all the way to Crossville and I think I just might have brought enough bullets to greet them properly." Rob was on a roll. "I do not appreciate the way folks have been treated in my territory and this was a nice way to get all of these SOBs to gather where I can educate them as to what behavior will be tolerated."

Ginger eased in alongside of the driver side of the semi. The others followed suit.

"Uh… Mister Flatford? What exactly is your territory? I thought you stayed North of Knoxville." David Munseizer asked.

"Today? Well today it's whatever I say it is. I'm thinkin' maybe all the way to Crossville. Depending, of course, on how fast a certain gunner goes through a couple hundred thousand rounds of ammo."

The Vulcans thundered over our heads as a rain of fire ripped through vehicles along both sides of the interstate.

Our speed had dropped, and I could see many targets approaching from the rear. They must have been happy to see that they were catching up until they saw the wreckage left by the semi. The majority took the exit at Harriman but about fifteen that continued to close the distance.

"Oh…Oh, I got this one," Rob said as he slipped into his own chair. "I don't like tailgaters."

I had the drones flying overhead so I got a clear view of the mini-rocket launchers that came into view as the doors slid open on the back of the trailer. There were nine stacked launchers with sixteen rockets in each. He emptied two of the launchers and thirty-two rockets flew to intercept the pursuing vehicles.

"This is the very reason I asked if Flatford was coming after us!" Bobby Tackett yelled. "I get him bein' out here, but why would the Hoods get involved?"

"I reckon when a bunch of sons of a bitches line up for fifty miles with the sole purpose of killin' my grandson, it's time to put the hood back on."

"Grandson? One of these mooks is your grandson?" I didn't catch which of the guys from the Knox Rail Savages asked.

Pop chuckled and pulled the trigger again on the Vulcans.

Bullets still peppered the driver side of the Vanguard, but they were fewer than before.

"Should have gone for the passenger side."

"Don't think I didn't notice the extra armor you had installed on this side. This side goes toward the bad guys." Ginger stayed right with the cab of the truck. "I hear you grumbling back there. Just shoot anything they miss."

"They ain't missin' much."

"Good. Did you know about this?"

"Nope, I figured we'd be dead before we got thirty miles out. Pop slipped this right by me."

"Well, aren't you just a ray of sunshine?" she asked.

"Just realistic. These bastards look like they run all the way to Crossville. I'm halfway through my ammo, already."

"They want us dead that badly?"

"They're just in it for the ratings," I said. "I bet the Hoods' ratings have gone through the roof. What do these coins and money symbols mean on the Clutch Stream? They're all over the place."

"Did you listen to anything I told you?"

I shrugged. "I guess not, if you talked about that."

"It's donations and sponsors. Coins are like fifty bucks and bills are hundreds."

"Damn," I said. "There's been a lot of 'em."

"How many?"

"Hell, I don't know. I been shootin' shit."

She giggled.

My drones topped the mountain we were crossing seconds before we did with the Vulcans still singing.

"I see the end of them!" Bolder yelled as I sent the image to them all.

"Still a bunch of 'em." I shook my head.

There had been almost every imaginable vehicle along the fifty miles from Knoxville to Crossville.

The Vulcans went silent.

"The good news is our speed has picked up," Flatford said. "But apparently 200,000 rounds of ammo wasn't quite enough to reach Crossville. Guess we'll just have to run over the rest of them." He strapped into the seat with a wide grin. "Rig for impact!"

"Jesus, this guy's crazy!" Samantha Sinn yelled.

"My kind of crazy!" her gunner, Lila Graves responded. "I love this guy!"

"Let's give them some room," Ginger said.

We spread out and took a position to the left of the rig as Charlie clipped the first car on the right, not much more than a rail buggy with an auto cannon mounted on it.

The front plate was designed like the guard on a locomotive, but it was still a little taller than the car, which crunched underneath the massive tires of the rig.

I saw the front guard lower.

"Of course it's movable." I chuckled.

I didn't have time to watch much more since we reached the first of the cars on the left and Ginger gave it a love tap on the rear fender, knocking the smaller car into a spin that impacted the car nearest it, sending them both over the embankment.

We rounded the last curve before Crossville with close to thirty different vehicles trying to get close enough to attack.

"Holy shit!"

The top of the semi-trailer erupted with fire and one of the Vulcans landed in the driver's side of a Timeshifter ... I think. It was hard to ID the thing with the twisted metal of a Vulcan where the driver would be.

"What the hell was that?"

Then my drones registered it.

"Is that a frackin' tank?"

Chapter 36

"Did he say a tank? Did you say tank?" Flatford was squirming in his chair. "Where?"

"Dead ahead!"

He laughed like a maniac. "Pop the top on this bitch, Larry! Pop the top!"

"What?"

"Hit the red button! The red one!"

"The one that says 'Never ever use'?"

"That's it! Punch it! I been waitin' my whole life for this!"

Pop hit the button and the tank fired again.

We were dropping in elevation, but I thought the shell had hit because a large section of the roof flew backwards to land in the cab of a truck. But the shell had been high. It actually hit one of the cars pursuing us.

Then my drones gave me a view of the top of the truck and the gun mounted there. It was every bit of twenty feet long

"What the hell kind of gun is that?"

"It's a BFG, Big Frackin' Gun. Larry, you can use elevation, but I never figured out a way to get a side movement with the hard mount."

Pop was hitting buttons. "Charlie, you gotta point us right at it!"

"It's pointing at us."

She swerved left just as the tank fired again. The shell clipped the top rear corner of the trailer but missed anything vital.

"Strapped for impact!"

The truck swung back in line with the tank.

"Just a little to the right, Charlie… almost there… Hold!"

It sounded like the world exploded as Pop pulled the trigger.

BRRRRRRRRRRRT

We shot out of the huge bank of smoke, but the semi didn't. The camera in the truck had went black.

The tank was an inferno.

"Pop!"

A few seconds later the truck rolled out of the smoke a lot slower than it was going before.

"Pop!"

The camera came back on to show flashing lights and smoke everywhere. Pop was helping Flatford out of his chair.

"Charlie?"

She groaned. "Still here. What did we hit?"

"I knew that bitch had a hell of a kick, but damn."

"What the hell did we just shoot with a kick that took us from sixty miles per hour to ten?"

"Salvaged it from an old airplane the military used to fly sixty years ago. It's called a GAU-8 Avenger."

"Rob, you're a frackin' psycho!" I yelled.

"I resemble that remark!"

"Yes, you do."

"Reckon we're done here, kid," Pop said. "Now go give 'em hell."

"Yes sir."

"What happened to the cars that were chasin' us," Bobby asked.

"I think they may have had enough," Lila said. "I know I would have been outta here after that. I think I'm in love."

"Reckon he's married, Lila."

"Damn it! Is it working though?"

I laughed. "Let's get the hell outta here before they decide to come back. Still got a long damn way to go."

The Clutch stream was going wild. There was a lot of comments about me being the grandson of Jeremy Hood. Coins and dollars rolled up the screen.

We passed the last exit to Crossville and my eye was drawn to the left of the road where it looked like a new ramp was added recently. The drones picked up movement.

"Move right! Move right!"

Ginger jerked the wheel to the right just as something caught the upper edge of the Vanguard's roof.

The drones showed the dragster as it took off. It was moving as fast as we were in an instant, but the ramp wasn't level with the interstate . . . so it topped the ramp and went airborne with autocannons firing.

The back wheel was what had caught the top edge of the roof. It sailed across three lanes and hit an old billboard. Something was highly flammable because the car ignited like a Roman candle and exploded.

"Has everybody in the world lost their frackin' minds?" Ginger muttered. "How did they think that would work?"

"If we hadn't swerved, it would have."

"The frack was that?" Bobby asked.

"Crossville crazies." I pulled a jar from the fridge.

The dash lit up with an alarm.

"Looks like we have a message from the Sponsors," I said.

"What is it?"

"They say we unlocked a perk by making it to Crossville. They set up a safe zone in Murfreesboro if we can reach it where we can rest and reload."

"It's probably a damned trap," Bobby said.

"Could be but I doubt it." I took a swallow from the jar. "They didn't expect us to get past that crazy shit back there and I doubt we would have without Flatford."

I was amazed there were nine teams left. Hell, I was amazed there were any.

"You're probably right. Let's put the hammer down and get there as quick as we can then."

I recalled the drone that was keeping an eye on the rig moving slowly up 127, with smoke still coming from the trailer in a couple of places.

Chapter 37

"Ellen, I'm not sure if I've ever seen anything quite like what we just witnessed today. I don't even know how the points will be distributed on this one."

"There were hundreds of cars out there. Will any of those points be attributed to the teams?"

"From what I can see, Flatford filled out the proper donation forms making every one of those bullets the property of the teams."

"I guess it will be up to the AADA how that is settled, Ellen. The big story of the moment is the revelation that at least one of the iterations of the Hoods was indeed the I-75 Butcher's grandfather. Because come on, we all knew they were different people over the years. I wonder which one he was."

"My bet is on one of the earliest. I remember when the Hoods' whole dynamic changed, and they went on a spree of success due to some very dynamic shooting abilities. Kelly was already a demon behind the wheel, but Jeremy changed. Multi-directional aiming was something they were well known for then. I believe we saw a lot of that same skill out there today."

"That was, what? Forty years ago, Ellen?"

"I'll hear no comments on age, Gavin."

He laughed. "I wouldn't dream of it, Ellen."

"What is your reaction with the revelation of a safe zone for them to recuperate in Murfreesboro?"

"To be brutally honest, Gavin, I don't think they ever planned for our intrepid car warriors to reach Crossville at all. Almost fifty miles of enemy combatants should have utterly destroyed them."

"Agreed, Ellen. I would ask what TTA is getting out of this but I'm watching the ratings since the Dead Man's Run began and I've never seen them so high. They've probably made enough from ads alone to buy those Gold Cross packages they supplied as a sign on bonus. This is reminiscent of the first days of autoduelling. We just might be witnessing the next evolution in entertainment. I'd guess that the Bolgeos are jumping for joy as the race continues."

We pulled over about halfway between Crossville and Cookeville. The drones were still in the air, and they would warn us of any incoming traffic.

"This is not good," Munseizer said as he kicked the loose armor on the passenger side of their Bombardier. "Heliadora is in some rough shape."

"You named your car Heliadora?"

"Of course." He pulled a hand welder from the car and tacked the armor back in place. "Not gonna help a whole lot. Can't do a full replace until we get to Murfreesboro."

"If we get to Murfreesboro."

I turned to Bobby to say something, but he was right.

"You got that right," Bolder said. "What's our plan?"

"I'd say we stick together and move as fast as we can." I said. "The drones are still good for a bit before chargin' so I think we can get as far as Lebanon before they have to charge. We'll have good coverage until then. Or I can rotate them and let one charge as the other two cover us."

"That makes better sense," Samantha said. "We have to get moving though, it's our only advantage."

"Agreed," I said. "Let's move."

"How bad is it?" Ginger asked as I got back into the Vanguard.

"Not good," I said as I donned the helmet again. "Every car has taken damage. Armor's lookin' pretty beat up. Maybe fifty percent left at best. We all took some hits."

"Some?"

I chuckled. "Alright, a lot of hits."

"How bad is Sascha?"

"Sascha?"

"Yes, our car."

"We're about in the same boat."

She frowned.

"Nothin' to be done," I said. "Let's kick this pig."

"Don't you be calling my Sascha a pig." She threw me a narrow eyed look and punched the throttle sending debris flying from the roadway in rooster tails.

My head was pushed back into the headrest as the Vanguard, Sascha, shot forward like a rocket.

Drone one dropped to attach itself to the roof on its charging port. Red lights blinked and I had to move it to port two before it would charge.

"Shit," I muttered.

My sensor range dropped as the drone went offline. They worked a lot better when all three were in the air.

"What is it?"

"One of the charger ports is damaged. Not gonna be able to charge all three drones at the same time."

"Think it's fixable?"

"I'm sure it is, just not by me. I just use 'em, not fix 'em. Maybe one of the others knows how."

Suddenly I lost the feed from drone two. Drone three tracked where the shot came from, and I shot a woman standing on top of a bluff holding a hunting rifle. I frowned as I watched her tumble down the cliff face. She hadn't shot at us, but we couldn't afford to lose the drones. She could have killed one of our drivers with shooting skills like that and she chose to shoot one of the drones. They were small for a reason, and she had still picked it off.

"What was that?"

"Lost a drone. Took out the sniper." I didn't think she needed to hear the details. The woman may have just been hunting… or she was purposefully taking out our sensor platform. I didn't have time to ascertain her motives.

My sensor range once again reduced in size.

"You did what?"

"Took out the sniper."

"Not you," she said. "Look at the clutch feed."

FinniusFreddy8675309 has sponsored you!

Two new Gelica Industries 400 drones incoming to the Murfreesboro safe zone for Blacktop Butchers courtesy of FinniusFreddy8675309! Uncle Al's Weapon Emporium thanks you for your business.

"Thanks Finnius Fred!" Ginger waved at the camera with a wide grin. "Sponsors like you are what keep us alive out here!"

That and the willingness to kill a girl for shooting what might have just been a random drone out of the sky.

Chapter 38

I relaunched the drone that was on charge as we neared Cookeville. Rumors abounded of the raiders that had moved in over the last year, so I expected attacks. What I didn't expect was close to fifty motorcycles.

"That's a Twisted H jacket," Bobby said. "They're some crazy bastards."

"It seems we have an overabundance of those today," Ginger said.

"You got that right, Red. I do have a little somethin' I was savin' for an emergency." He responded. "Let's see how well they do on oil."

Sensors showed bikes sliding and crashing all over the road behind us.

"Good one, Bobby."

Half of the bikes were out of it but there were still a bunch of them incoming. I sent a suggestion and got affirmatives from the rest. We split and braked hard. All twenty five bikes shot past us and we accelerated again.

"Run em down. That's what these ram plates are made for."

I saw a Spider in the bunch with rear rockets like my bike and I hit it with the buffalo gun and scanned the others. Most of them had front faced weapons. One other had a rear rocket and got one shot off before the Painted Ladies fired their own buffalo gun and the rider lost a large portion of his upper body. The rocket impacted the road in front of Primal Rage, but Southard managed to swerve out of most of the explosion. They still took some damage on the right front of their Dragon.

Armor exploded from the right quarter panel.

Ginger was a little hesitant to hit the first bike that came within range, but Larry Southard was not. He hit one of the bikes at full speed and sent the rider flying through the air.

A bullet hit the window almost in front of Ginger and she floored the Vanguard. The biker that had shot the windshield hit the ground and I felt the thump on the bottom of the car as we went over top of him. Hitting someone on a motorcycle was a whole lot different than tapping a car and sending it off the road. She was used to racing on the track and being aggressive with cars, but motorcycles were different. But when they are shooting at you, you do what you have to.

I saw another motorcycle with a rear-mounted weapon and fired the buffalo gun once more.

The Painted Ladies and Rutledge Rippers sandwiched a biker between their cars with a crunch. As they separated two more bikes were hit by the ram plates on their vehicles.

"Incoming!" I yelled as a large vehicle plowed through the guard rail and jumped the embankment. It was an enormous pickup truck on huge tires like they used to have in the monster truck rallies. It landed directly on top of the Rutledge Rippers Joseph Special and crushed the top in on Jack Hill and Deborah Gillis. The bikes had slowed us down enough for the monster truck to get to us.

"Punch it!" I yelled.

I was pushed back into the seat again as Ginger accelerated, the others following suit. I turned my buffalo gun toward the monster truck and put one round straight through the engine into the driver.

The Twisted H bikers decided they'd had enough and fled back toward the exit they'd come from.

I brought my drone around and focused on the Ripper's car. Both of them were dead and so was the guy who'd done it, so there wouldn't be a bounty to collect. I may not have been able to stop them from being killed, but I could sure stop their killer from collecting a bounty.

We left Cookeville with one less team than we entered.

"Fracking monster truck…" Bobby muttered on coms.

"This just keeps getting weirder and weirder," Lila said.

"You got that right," Tina Maples of the Sevierville Slammers said.

I hadn't heard much from the Slammers since we'd hit the road, but Tina Maples and Rob York in their modified Rockwell seemed pretty solid. They were both experienced duellists with more experience than most of the pack. I'd been expecting them to try to take over the leadership, but they seemed happy to follow my lead. Perhaps because of the sensor suite. Our Vanguard had the best sensor package of all the others thanks to the sponsor who had supplied it. The drones were a big part of that.

"I have to pull in one of the drones to charge," I said. "Everybody needs to look sharp while our coverage is smaller."

"We'll keep our eyes peeled," Bobby said.

I pulled in the back drone and let it settle into the charger as Ginger put on more speed.

She was quieter than normal as we streaked down I-40 toward Lebanon.

"You had to do it," I said. "It's never easy."

She remained quiet but she nodded her head.

We barely slowed down as we tore through Lebanon. I expected an attack that didn't come. We slowed long enough to take the off ramp onto I-840 that bypassed Nashville, which had been abandoned years ago. It had taken a lot of damage in the bad times and had fallen into complete ruin after that. I figured there were a few gangs left in the area, but most people wouldn't even try it with the roads destroyed and the majority of the buildings collapsed.

Our designated route didn't call for us to try to get through Nashville though.

"Surprised it wasn't," I muttered.

"What?" Ginger asked.

"Nothin'. Just surprised they didn't make us go through Nashville instead of around."

"Bite your tongue."

"True enough. Don't want to jinx it."

"No doubt."

"Frack! Too late." I toggled switches. "Lookout guys, my drone just went down."

"Can't run this fast without coverage," Bobby said.

We dropped down to about sixty miles per hour from the one twenty we had been doing.

My regular sensors flickered.

"Shit! Heads on swivels!"

I looked to my left and flinched as I saw the dump truck. It missed us and the following cars in our diamond formation, except the last three.

I heard a scream on the coms just before the truck plowed into the side of the Painted Ladies. Damage Inc and the Tacketts impacted the truck as well and all three were slammed off the road.

My sensors came back online, and the missing drone crossed over the wreckage where a whole horde of people with the blue body paint of the Speedway Cannibals dragged our people, struggling from their cars.

I groaned as they dragged them toward hidden vehicles.

"How bad is it?" Ginger asked.

We were already several miles past them. "Pull over. Sensors show a Quarry up ahead. Pull off the road there."

Chapter 39

"We're twenty minutes from the safe zone," Rob York of the Slammers said. "Nothing we can do for them. We're not stopping."

Ginger slowed and eased to the side of the road.

"Sorry guys," Pat Keller of the Knox Rail Savages said as they streaked past.

The Magnolia Madness team didn't say a word as they followed the other two.

I pointed to the side of the road at the quarry road. "Let's get down into that and get to those buildings over there."

Ginger didn't hesitate. She ran through the fence on the side of the road and turned down the gravel road leading down into the quarry.

I looked back to see Southard follow us. I was breathing hard as I fought with myself over what needed to happen.

"What is it, Jake? Are you hit?"

For a moment I relived two of the worst days I had ever faced. A calm settled over me as I made my decision.

"No, I'm good."

We pulled into the front of what looked like some sort of headquarters for the quarry.

I scanned the area with the sensors. There was a single person in the small trailer.

Stepping out of the car, I could see the heat signature just inside the door.

"Come on out! Hands better be empty!"

The door opened slowly, and two hands stuck out the opening before it opened all the way. An older guy with dirt stained work clothes stepped out.

"Don't shoot me!"

"Not plannin' on it, old timer. Just keep your hands away from that scattergun beside the door."

He looked a little surprised that I had known about it, but he kept his hands out front as he stepped out of the trailer and down the stairs.

"You're those guys from the TV," he said. "That big race."

"We are." I said as Larry climbed out of the driver side of their Dragon.

Smoke started rolling from somewhere in the back and Jon jumped out of it as well. Something sparked and flashed.

"Shit!" Bolder slammed the door shut. "Frackin' Power Plant! That's it! She's as good as dead."

I let out a long breath. Ginger had a worried look.

I pointed toward a dirt bike leaned against the building. "That run?"

"Yessir."

"Got any other weapons around here?"

"Just my old double barrel."

"You planning on going back?" Southard looked dumbfounded.

"You saw the drone footage. They dragged 'em out alive."

"Yeah?"

"I wouldn't be worried if they'd been killed. Gold Cross brings 'em back. You don't even remember anything past your last download. But they're gonna do some awful things to them. They're gonna rape, torture, and eat all of them on national television. It'll be everywhere they go. No escapin' what that'll do to a person."

"All true."

"Well I can't abide that. I'm goin' back there. If we're not back here in a couple hours, I need you and Bolder to make sure she gets to Murfreesboro. If we're not there by morning we're not coming."

"Hold on a damned minute!" Ginger exploded. "No way in hell do you go in there!"

I placed my hands on her shoulders. "You have to go on. You can't quit."

I turned to the guy from the trailer. "No weapons huh?"

"No weapons. I got some dynamite, though."

I grinned. "Now that sounds interestin'. Let's go take a look."

Ginger stepped back in front of me. "You really think I'm just gonna ride off?"

My hand touched her face and lightly pushed a stray lock back. "If you don't you may be violatin' that contract. We did all this for you to get that Gold Cross. Don't give it up."

"What about you? You have the same contract."

"You need it to survive. I don't. I need to know you'll go so I can do what I need to. They don't deserve what's gonna happen to 'em. I've been there and I can't let it happen again."

"There were hundreds of them, Jake."

"And they deserve what's about to happen."

"What are you going to do with that many?"

"Reckon I'll kill 'em." I turned back to the old man. "Let me get a look at that dynamite."

The camera drone that followed our car dropped closer and followed me as the old man led me to a locked shed.

I pointed at it. "I'm talkin' to the operator behind this camera. You follow me in there, you better keep out of sight. If you give me away, I swear to God, I'll hunt you down and cut your frackin' throat. My contract says I have to deal with these drones but I'm about to do some secret squirrel shit. You got that?"

The drone tilted down in the front just like a nod.

I followed the old man into the shed.

"Remember, two hours. The lag between live and broadcast will be gone, and everyone knows where you are." I put my tablet inside of my body armor. "Be gone before then."

I kickstarted the dirt bike.

I twisted the throttle and sent the bike forward with a rooster tail of gravel peppering the building. As I reached the interstate, I placed the tablet on a mount between the handlebars.

"D2."

The picture on the tablet showed the view from the drone I had attached to the tablet. It was at a high enough range it wouldn't have any issue with the cannibals. They weren't jamming now that they wanted the cameras to see what they did to the teams.

I accelerated and shot north on I-840 until I reached the first cross road. The sky was darkening as a storm came rolling in from the west.

"Nice," I muttered. "More cover."

I turned left on Mona Road and accelerated again. Then I stopped at the crossing with Bill France Blvd. There was a lot of open ground ahead and the bike was loud. I parked it in the woods and took my tablet from the handlebars.

Zooming in on the raceway, I could see the camera drones hovering out in front of crowded grandstands.

"Guess they all want to see the show," I said in disgust.

Since the speedway had shut down a lot of undergrowth had sprouted in what used to be open fields and a bunch of ramshackle buildings were scattered around what looked like an old sports bar. You could still barely read the sign that said Nashville Cars and Coffee.

Two camera drones registered inside of the bar.

I growled and turned toward my camera. "Sam and Lila?"

The camera bounced again.

"Stay low and follow me. Remember what I said."

It nodded.

I ducked low and moved through the brush toward the bar at a pretty good clip. Some were in the ramshackle tent city but at least half of them were already in the grandstands for the show. Except for whoever was in the bar with the girls. I hoped I was fast enough.

I snaked between some of the shabby outbuildings and used my tablet to check the area ahead.

There was a sentry outside of the bar, so I eased into the shadows at the back of the bar and crept around to peek past the corner. The guy had blue body paint that looked like it was applied by the handful. He was smoking a cigarette and looking the other way. My left hand snaked around his neck to lift his chin while my right pulled my knife across his throat, careful to make sure to get the carotid. Smoke from the cigarette billowed from his throat as the pressure from my left hand pulled the wound open.

I glanced over to see the camera drone. My eyes narrowed and the drone shot back around the corner.

Chapter 40

I let the cannibal slide to the ground, took his rifle, checked the feed, and slipped through the front door. The front room was empty, but I heard noises from the back.

"Leave her alone!" I thought it was Lila's voice. "You fracking bastard!"

I looked around the room and saw a large axe leaning against the door. With a grim smile I leaned the rifle on the door frame and picked up the axe. Normally I wouldn't trade down in weaponry. Any weapon is to be used to get a better weapon, but I didn't need to announce my presence with gunfire either.

I heard a loud smack as I stepped inside of the back room. "Your turn will be soon."

I stepped around a shelf just inside of the supply room.

Samantha Sinn was chained to a wall in front of a large blue painted man. He was removing his belt as I stepped closer. Lila was in a cage in the corner of the room and saw me just before the axe sank from the crook of his shoulder to his spine. He started to scream, and I yanked him backward with the axe. Impacting the floor knocked my axe loose. Blood spurted all the way across the room.

Sam's top was ripped most of the way off and her head rose to see me instead of the cannibal. Her left eye was swelling where the man had struck her.

"Turner?"

"Yeah," I said and stomped the screaming man's throat. The screaming stopped with a gurgle. I started rifling through the dying man's pockets.

"Keys in the desk over there," Lila said.

"You came back?" Sam asked as I yanked the drawers open until I found them.

I unlocked the chain manacles from Sam and went to the cage. It took a couple of tries before I found the right key. I looked over with a scowl at the camera drones in the corner that had been recording.

"I'll tell you the same as I did him." I pointed at the drone that followed me in. "You frack around and give away my position, I swear to God I'll hunt you down."

The drones turned their cameras toward the other drone which was bobbing vigorously.

I pulled my tablet from my armor and studied the screen. There were a lot of them at the grandstands but there were almost as many scattered among the tents and ragged buildings between the bar and the track. There were six stakes in the area in front of the stands. Four were occupied by my teams. They were tied to the stakes with a lot of wood piled around them.

"Really?"

"What?" Sam asked as she pulled her top back together as best she could.

I showed her the drone footage.

"Yeah, they showed us that before dragging us here for what they planned for us."

I growled and slipped the tablet inside my armor.

"Follow me and keep low. That goes for you too." I pointed at the drones.

I picked up the rifle I saw laying with the dead man's shirt. Stepping out of the room, I picked up the rifle I'd left by the door and handed it back to Lila.

Sam looked at me with an eyebrow raised.

"Gunner gets first gun."

"Fair enough."

I stepped out of the bar with my rifle at the ready. Rain was starting to fall, and the sky was darkening. Motioning for them to follow, I slipped around the corner and toward the occupied tents.

Just before reaching them I saw a large propane tank. I changed direction and opened the top of the tank when I reached it to see it was half full.

"Gas companies will sell to anyone, I guess," Lila whispered.

"Suits me." I pulled a package from my pack.

"Jesus, where'd you get that?"

"New sponsor."

I placed the package below the tank and flipped the switch on.

"What else you got in there?"

"Two more of these and a detonator switch."

"Holy hell," she said pointing toward the left. "I saw some fuel tanks for the cars over there."

"Excellent."

She grinned. "Frack these sons of bitches."

I moved toward where she had indicated and soon enough, we were approaching several large tanks. Around the tanks, there were a bunch of vehicles, including a dump truck with a torn-up front end.

"If we'd been in regular cars, we'd be dead already," Sam whispered as we passed the truck.

Someone stepped around the front of the truck and stopped as he saw us. Sam let her shirt fall open and his eyes shifted to her. I threw my knife which sank to the hilt into his throat. I was seconds behind it and slammed him to the ground. I almost severed his head as I yanked the knife across and out.

His body stilled in moments.

"Damnit, man," Lila whispered. "You better put those away, Sam. Deadly weapons."

I glanced up as she closed her top again. "Might wanna keep 'em ready, though."

She grinned.

I slipped behind the fuel tanks and attached another bomb. Then ran across a small clearing to plant the third on a second fuel tank. The dump truck was a diesel, but a lot of the vehicles were gas. There was a tank of racing fuel between the two others, and I suspected my bombs would take that too along with most of the cars and trucks.

"Stay low and stay back for this part," I said.

Returning to the man I'd killed, I took a hatchet from his side and hung it on a loop of my vest. Sam had already taken his rifle and they followed me toward the shanties.

The first tent I came to, I slipped inside and yanked a blue-skinned man's head back as he was about to take a drink of beer. My knife slid across his throat, and I dropped him to grab a dumbstruck, blue-faced woman by her hair and plunge the knife into her neck.

I stepped back out of the tent with blood splattered on my face and clothes.

Lila and Sam both looked inside and back at me with eyes wide. It hadn't taken me long and the bodies still twitched.

I held another knife in my left hand now and moved toward the next one with rain washing blood off of me in little rivulets.

Chapter 41

"They've been promising what they would do over the last few months, Ellen! It looks like our racers are in serious trouble, now!"

"That's right, Gavin. The Speedway Cannibals announced their intentions after they took residence—"

"I can't do it, Ellen! We're about to go live, ladies and gents!"

"Are you sure that's a good idea, Gavin?"

"I think it's a great idea, Ellen! Folks, you just saw the Speedway Cannibals capture three of our racing teams. We are going live to give you a shot of what's going down as we speak!"

I left the last of the ramshackle huts with blood coating my clothes and face. I entered with two knives and left with a pair of Viking hand axes attached to my armor.

"Jesus, Turner."

"Now we go get our team."

I unslung the rifle I had stolen and made sure I could reach all of the magazines. "When it starts, I want you to go free our boys and get the hell out of there."

"What about the pile of cannibals watching the show?" Lila asked.

"They're gonna be busy."

Both nodded.

I stepped around the corner of the shack and raised my rifle.

The giant screen across from the grandstand showed blue skinned people dragging our guys from the cars. I didn't realize it had been that long.

"We are going live to give you a shot of what's going down as we speak!"

The screen broke down into three screens as the first shot straight down onto a large blue-skin in a stage in front of all the others. The second screen showed four stakes with our team tied up. The third was a shot from behind me as I took aim.

The blue-skin on stage stopped and cocked his head to the side as he saw the third scene. Then his head flew backward with his blood and brains splashing across Bobby Tackett.

"Holy shit, Billy! Is that…?"

"Tazewell! Damnit, Bobby, it's Tazewell!"

I stepped out where I could aim and set the rifle on auto. I raked the fire across the crowded stands until my gun emptied. Ejecting the mag, I slammed another home and continued spraying.

"Bobby! Tazewell came to play!"

"I can't see, where is he?"

I ejected another mag and moved to the right to keep their attention so the girls could get to the captives. I drove the new mag into the bottom of the rifle and kept moving. I sprayed all across the crowd. I didn't need to kill them all, I just needed to make it hurt. People don't want to fight when they've been shot.

"Bobby, if we get outta this, I'm moving to Tazewell!"

"You hate Tazewell, Billy!"

"I don't anymore, Bobby! I love that son o' ma bitch!"

My hand landed on an empty slot where my last magazine had rested. A large group charged out of the rain toward me, and I drew my hand cannon. The front three went down and I threw the pistol to impact a fourth right between the eyes. He dropped like a poled ox. They were about six feet out and I drew the pair of axes.

There were six men left in the group and I raked the axe across one's midsection and circled to the left to keep him between me and the others. As he toppled, my left-hand axe hit another in the knee, separating the joint altogether. His bat hit across my left shoulder and pain shot through me. I couldn't let it distract me, so I pushed it aside and brought my right axe around to hit the left side of another's neck.

"Jesus, Billy! Watch that son o' ma bitch go!"

The last of the group was down, and I looked up at the screen. It was focused on me, and I stood blood-covered in the rain amongst a bloody mess of dead and dying men with my axes dripping red. Another large group got out of the stands, and I tripped a switch on my arm. Explosions rocked the speedway.

A bunch of the blue-skins fled but there was still a group of twenty or so that ran in our direction. I glanced back and saw that the girls were cutting ropes, but I needed to give them more time.

I wished I'd told her I loved her. I didn't deserve it after the things I've done, but I would have loved to see her again. Maybe the other me would feel like he could start a new life.

I met them in the middle of the field and cut down the first one with the axe in my right hand. I barely got the left up enough to block a swinging bat. It still sent a stab of pain through me. Up to this moment I was cold and calculating but a wave of rage swept through me, and adrenaline filled my body. Ignoring the pain, I went berserk.

The next moments were a haze of rage. I found myself in a spot where none were near me, even though I still faced ten or so men. I was still screaming in fury with fire in my veins. I heard a powerful hum of electric drives and glimpsed red hair as the Vanguard sent bodies flying.

The fury was gone as quickly as it had come, and my vision blurred. I saw an angel as I dropped to my knees and lost my grip on the axes. The angel came closer and closer.

"You're here…" I muttered as strong arms caught me from behind.

"I forgot to ask you," Southard said. "How do you get to Murfreesboro? I could've sworn that's where we were but then shit started blowing up."

Chapter 42

"Maybe you shouldn't have blown everything up, Tazewell," Bobby said pointing at the wreckage where all of the cars had been parked. "Looks like the only thing left is that."

I laughed which hurt. You can only do so much with superglue and duct tape. The safe zone in Murfreesboro was the old St. Thomas Hospital. If we could get there, a few of the cuts would need stitches

We drove out of the speedway in the Vanguard and an ancient Volkswagen minibus with flowers painted all over it. Bobby honked the horn as we drove out and held his left hand out the window making a rude gesture.

Billy held his right hand out the other side with the same gesture. A couple of blue-skins were running down the road and Bobby ran right over them.

I shrugged and winced. "Frack 'em."

It was still raining when we reach the interstate. I slipped my helmet on and launched the drones that had been charging while we were prepping to leave.

"You guys hang back further than before," I said. "That minibus ain't got no armor."

"Don't have to tell me twice, boss," Bobby answered as the minibus dropped back.

I left one of the drones centered on the bus so that I could keep an eye on them. This was going to be the hardest part of making it to Murfreesboro. We were going to have to keep that bus alive.

As we passed the quarry, I looked down at the main headquarters where there were several cars now.

"I hope that old man's all right," I said. "I never did get his name."

"Dennis," Ginger said. "He said most people call him Old Man Dennis. He said he was getting the hell out of there as soon as we left."

"Good."

She kept her speed down, so the bus didn't drop too far behind.

"Wreckage ahead," I said. "That overpass."

I brought the drone down to get a closer look and saw two familiar cars. There was no one else near the cars. The drone got closer and saw the bodies inside of the cars.

"That's the Magnolia Madness and the Knox Rail Savages." I sent the drone higher and scanned the area. "Doesn't look like there's anybody left hangin' around. They must've pursued the Slammers."

I took a jar from the beer fridge and took a long drink. Now the pain was growing, and I didn't need to be distracted by it. "Let's move on. Looks safe enough for the minibus."

"What's everybody so worried about? We run into anybody, we'll just throw Jake at 'em." Bobby said. "If there's a bunch, we'll give him an axe."

Somebody snorted. "Dude's got some anger issues."

"I don't think I wanna do that again," I said.

"Neither do I," Sam replied. "That was a close one."

"I don't know," Bobby said. "First time I ever had to be rescued and it was by a hot chick with her ti … womanly assets hanging out. It hasn't been as bad of an experience as you'd think."

"Yeah, but I was tied the other way and all I saw was some dude choppin' up blue-skins," Billy responded. "I didn't get to see any ti … womanly assets."

"That doesn't seem fair. Hey, Billy."

The minibus swerved a couple of times.

"Sam, I thought I told you to keep those things holstered," Lila said. "Deadly weapons."

"Fair is fair, Lila."

I laughed again and it hurt just as much as the other time. Ginger was looking at me through the rearview.

"Thanks, Gin. You saved my ass out there."

She gave a small nod and then looked back at the road.

"More wreckage," I said. "Doesn't look like the Slammers, though. Maybe they got through and took out these guys. I always got the impression they were pretty tough. And that old Rockwell station wagon reminds me of Pop's Conestoga."

"They refused to stop."

"I can't really blame 'em, to be honest. If I hadn't lived that scenario personally, I don't know if I would've stopped either. Most people don't have that kind of experience and know what it is to live it. They're back there, joking about it because it's the only way to deal with it. It helps that they just almost lived it."

"I can't even imagine what you went through."

"I survived it. Can you imagine watching on television as that happened to the previous you?"

She shuddered. "What the hell are we doing out here Jake?"

"Surviving, Gin. That's all we can do right now." I hit the com. "Looks like the Slammers cleared these. You guys can come on up. That far one looks like a buffalo gun. I want to see if there's any ammo left."

"I'll check it for you, you look like a mummy running around with all those bandages on you. Stay in the car." Munseizer got out of the passenger side of the minibus and dug around in the wreckage. He dragged a large canister out of the Tonto.

Driver and gunner were riddled with bullets.

"That's from an assault rifle," Munseizer said as he handed the canister in the side door of the Vanguard. "I'm guessing the Slammers are out of ammo for the big gun. Not sure why they didn't scavenge this unless there're more still chasing them."

"Could be." I took the canister with a wince.

"Just let me load your canister, you crazy bastard. Cut all over and still trying to do it all. You got three more gunners that can be doing this."

"He's right, Jake. Let one of them run the weapons til we get to Murfreesboro. You break that glue loose, and you'll bleed out."

We took the next few minutes to get my ass back out of the Vanguard gunner seat and into the minibus.

"Best gunner?"

"Lila or Bolder," Billy said immediately.

Bobby looked at him askance.

"Agreed," Oscar Polk said.

"Truth is the truth," Billy said. "I've been watching."

"One of you needs to take my spot in the Vanguard."

Lila pointed at Bolder. "Go."

Bolder got out of the minibus and I eased into the seat he had vacated.

"You'll be better off lying down in the middle there," Lila said. "You're bleeding again. Let me check the wounds. I may have to put more superglue on it. I was a nurse's aide a long time ago. Don't you worry, Ginger. We'll take care of him."

I must have passed out a short time after that.

A familiar boom woke me up. It was the buffalo gun firing. I was halfway sitting up with my hand cannon in my hand before someone pushed me back down.

"Don't worry, it's already over."

I let my hand cannon drop back to my side as I stared straight up at Sam's chest while she held me down.

"Not that I'm complainin' about the view, but I'm alright now."

"Deadly weapons, Sam," Lila said. "There was a sniper in one of the buildings. Bolder took him out."

"We're just a few minutes out from the safe zone," Bobby said. "Looks like the Slammers came through here. Couple of wrecks ahead, looks like their armor is crushed. Wonder if the Slammers are out of ammo completely. At least they cleared the way for us."

"There's the wall, Bobby!"

Bobby blew the ridiculous high pitched horn twice as we drove through the gate behind the Vanguard. I could see several guards on the wall waving at us.

Chapter 43

"We should probably put you out," the nurse said. "Or I can do local area anesthetics. There're a lot of wounds going by the amount of duct tape."

"Area." I shook my head. "Can't be out. We don't have enough time for that."

"It's not long term."

"Can't trust 'em."

"Your team?"

"No." I pointed at the camera hovering outside of the room.

They refused to let it in with me and I was just fine with that.

"Soon as I go out the powers that be would probably take away the safe zone."

"These guards are our men," she said. "You are safe here."

"Better stick with the local anesthetics, anyway."

"Will do." She caught the edge of one of the pieces of duct tape. "This is probably going to hurt." She pointed at the long scar down my chest with her other hand. "But it sure won't hurt worse than that did. That looks pretty awful."

"It was pretty awful," I said. "Let's get this done."

I grunted as she ripped the tape off of the first one.

Surprisingly, most of the wounds didn't need stitches. The superglue was holding just fine. She applied tape across the superglue to give it added support. Two of them needed stitches quite badly, though. They were a bit deeper. A rule I had learned a long time ago about knife fights was expect to get stabbed. They're brutal. Knives are good for secret squirrel shit, sneaking up and taking someone out silently. By the time you are in an actual fight, you better have something better than a knife. I prefer to have a gun and shoot them from a distance. It hurts a lot less.

I was starting to feel again in the places where the nurse put stitches and it was uncomfortable. Uncomfortable but bearable. If not for the body armor I had been wearing, things would've been much worse.

I looked around for my clothes, but they were gone. I was sitting there in a pair of shorts when Ginger walked into the room carrying a stack of clothes.

"You wouldn't believe how many drones have been dropping off packages since we got here! Clothes, body armor, weapons, ammo, and even that pair of drones for Sascha."

She paused, taking in the various bandages.

"I didn't realize there were so many when Lila was patching you up."

"Couple needed stitches," I said.

She laid the clothes down.

"Gin, I need to talk to you."

"Me too." She sat down beside me.

"I was out there in the middle of that and all I could think about was you. I love you, Gin, and I was afraid I'd never get the chance to say it."

"You don't think I know that, you big dumbass. Why else are you out here traipsing through hell for me. I was thinking I'd let you run off and not told you the same. I love you, Jake Turner."

"But you've seen what I am …"

She held a finger up. Then picked up the remote for the TV on the wall and turned it on. There was a news anchor speaking but the screen behind him was from my camera as I went through that ramshackle tent city.

"They've played this footage nonstop since we got here. We've all seen it."

"I didn't give 'em a chance, Gin. I just killed 'em. I don't even know if they participated."

"They declared war on us before we even started this race. They announced on TV that they planned on catching every one of us and eating us on national television. This is a war, Jake, and they were the enemy."

"How can you love someone who can do something like that?"

"The same way women have loved soldiers throughout history, with all my heart."

Then she was in my arms, our lips met, and for a little while everything was right in the world.

Sometime later, she left to help install the drones into our car and I laid there in a daze. I really didn't expect her to be able to accept what I'd done. She knew it all now and she didn't run away.

As I began to get dressed, one of the guards stepped inside the room. There were no cameras allowed inside this part of the hospital.

"Sir?"

"You don't have to call me sir," I said. "What can I do for you?"

He pointed at the television. "Everybody's seen what you did for your teammates. That was some deep blue hero shit."

"I couldn't just drive away," I said.

"That's what I'm talking about, sir. I have a cousin who works for the networks. He's a cameraman. In fact he is a cameraman behind one of your personal cameras."

"He did right by me if he's the one who followed me into that," I said. "He stayed low and didn't give away my position just like I told him to do. I know it wasn't his fault that the network went live right in the middle of it, so he doesn't have to worry about me."

"That'll probably make him sleep a little better." The guard grinned. "But that's not exactly why I'm here." .

"Do tell."

"You guys are in a pretty rough situation, and I think I can help."

"We can use all the help we can get. What do you have in mind?"

"That depends on how risky you're willing to go."

"This whole thing's been a massive crapshoot," I said. "We're already twice as far as I expected to get."

"Then I think you may like this."

Chapter 44

"Everybody be quiet, we can't talk about him, now. He just came in."

I chuckled as I closed the door to the cafeteria behind me. Everyone was clustered around a long table in the center of the room except for Tina Maples and Rob York, the Sevierville Slammers. They were at a table by themselves in the far corner.

I walked across the room and stop beside their table. "You guys don't have to sit way over here."

"It's all right, kid," Rob said. "I can admit when I chose the wrong path."

"Nobody in their right mind would've stopped," I said.

"You stopped. You went back."

"I never claimed to be in my right mind."

"I don't think they want us over there," Tina said. "We're out of this anyway. Our car is shot. And I don't think we'll have any sponsors drop us off anything after that."

"If you want to quit, feel free. But I think we've got a way to continue with everyone if you want to come. The only caveat I have is we go forward as a team. One team. Old-style Three Musketeers shit, all for one and one for all. You down for that?"

"You're damn right I am," Rob said. "Tina, what do you think?"

She nodded.

"Then come and join us for dinner. Afterwards we'll have a little strategy session."

"How did your popularity score just go up?" Southard asked. "You just walked into the damn room."

He looked up from his tablet as the Slammers followed me back across the room.

"Oh."

"They just did what many of us would've done in their shoes," I said. "But here we're startin' fresh."

Ginger sat across the table from where I stood with a small grin on her face.

I rounded the table, sat beside her in one of the empty chairs, and motioned toward the other open seats. The table was originally set up for twenty-four people and the lack of many was glaring. Half of the seats remained empty.

I pointed at the empty seats. "This is what happens when we don't work together. First Thunder Road and the Sons of Liberty chose to ignore what the majority of us were focused on. This was their right, but it cost 'em. Hell, it cost 'em everything. Rob Flatford and the Hoods gave us an opportunity to survive the initial gauntlet and he gave us time to begin working together. Even after we started working together, we lost the Twin Terrors. I can't fault the Slammers, Rippers, and Savages for driving on."

"It cost us dearly," Tina said. "At this point we're out of the race."

I looked at the cameras that were focused on us. "Maybe. After dinner we're going to have a strategy session." I pointed at the cameras. "Without any observation. As for right now, this looks like real meat sitting in front of us. Let's enjoy that for a moment."

"Not to mention, you gave us a chance to not get murdered," Lila said.

"And possibly worse," Sam added.

"I really wasn't looking forward to the bonfires." Bobby forked a piece of beef onto his plate. "Being eaten by blue-skinned cannibals is not at the top of my list of ways that I want to go out. I was thinking more along the lines of an incoming rocket or something like that. Maybe a blaze of glory. Definitely not on a dinner plate."

"I didn't see any plates," Munseizer said. "I think it was probably going to be one of those 'pick off a piece at a time' scenarios."

"That might even be worse." Billy took a piece of beef and placed it on his plate as well.

"Doesn't seem to be slowing anybody down on digging into that roast," Lila said.

"It's beef." Polk loaded his plate. "How often do we get that?"

"True enough," Lila replied. "Pass that platter down this way."

I saw a crooked smile on Sam's face when she saw Ginger lean into my side as she finished what she put on her plate. My arm felt natural as I laid it across her shoulders. I remembered many a day just sitting with her nestled in at my side. They were better days in a better time, and I truly hoped I would see those days again when this was done. At the least, the new me might get a chance to live those days again.

As the last of them finish their plates, I motioned toward a guard.

"Yes?"

"Any chance we can get some privacy in here for a strategy session without any cameras? We can move to a place already designated if you want."

"It's no problem, sir."

He strode across the room to the camera drones and herded them out the door. He nodded at me as he closed the doors. We had the room completely to ourselves.

"All right, man, what's this plan you got in mind?" Bobby asked.

"While I was in the hospital room a certain guard came to visit." I took my tablet from my shirt and laid it on the table. "Now because this guy is a guard, I don't want to bring him in here and risk the chance that the cameras catch him."

"All right."

"Seems this fella has a brother that owns a shop about three blocks from here and he's interested in providing a sponsorship to all of us. You're all familiar with the build of our Vanguard. It's a rocket on wheels. This guy is willing to provide us a way to use that speed to the greatest advantage. The downside of this? What vehicle can keep up with that rocket on wheels at full speed?"

"You're talking bikes," Munseizer said.

"I am."

"Bikes are a hard sell in the arena," he said. "But think how far we can go in the two hours before anybody knows we have them."

"That's what I'm thinkin'. We can be halfway to Memphis before they even know we're gone." I pushed the spot on my tablet to show where the bike shop was located. "Now Derek has told me he can provide us a way to get out of here, unseen by anyone except our cameras, which will have the two-hour delay. The moment we leave here we're on a timer."

"It's not like we have much choice," Lila said. "All of our cars are gone. What have we got left? A VW flower bus? You saw the contract as well as we did. You can't quit. Succeed or die."

"You could still quit," I said. "You just lose the Gold Cross package."

"We all know why you're here. They certainly made everyone aware when you won Amateur Night. You turned around and risked all of that to come get us. Don't think that the Corporation wouldn't have violated your contract if you'd failed. Because technically you quit and went back. Your success was the only thing that kept your current contract from being violated."

Bobby was speaking in a completely serious tone, which didn't happen very often.

He pointed at Ginger. "This whole thing for you was to be able to live on after ALS was done with you. And you turned around and followed him, technically, violating your contract. You're both a couple of idiots, but you're glorious idiots, and I'm going with you whether anyone else does or not."

"I'm with him." Billy pointed at his brother.

"I'm in," Lila said. "I'm still holding out for a chance to convince that Flatford guy he needs a second wife. Not sure he would go for that if I abandon you right now."

"Saved us from an ugly death, Turner." Sam nodded. "I'm in."

"After our last decision, I have a lot to make up for. I'm in." Rob slapped the table.

"Me too," Tina added.

"I've wanted a bike since I was a kid." Bolder had a far off look in his eye.

Southard laughed at him. "I reckon if they're just giving them away…"

"Every one of you is insane," Oscar Polk said. "My kind of people. Hell, yeah."

"We're all fracking idiots." Munseizer shook his head. "So what kind of bikes does he have?"

I slipped the tablet over to them, where he could see the name of the shop.

"Tornados?"

"He's a Tornado dealer but he may have some used bikes of other brands. Not sure what he's going to offer us, but Derek guarantees they will be high-speed bikes. Bikes that'll keep up with the Vanguard."

"Damn. How fast is that Vanguard?"

"We're not even sure."

Chapter 45

I didn't want to leave the room. Ginger was nestled under my arm, and I didn't want to move.

She sighed. "Time to go do it."

"I know." I reluctantly stood up.

We'd been in the safe zone for six hours and we were scheduled for another six before we had to leave. Ginger and I met everybody at the Vanguard.

"Timer starts now," I said. "Load up."

I took my place in the gunner chair of the Vanguard as Ginger got into the driver's seat. Everyone else piled in the VW flower bus. Our cameras floated alongside.

"Let's hit it."

Derek, the guard who had talked to me, opened the gate and we eased out with no lights on. It was close to dusk, and we would be using the night as a cover. I launched the drones as we left the gate and kept a close eye on my HUD. They were depending on me, so I was going to try my best.

We turned right on Medical Center Parkway, heading back toward the interstate, covering the three blocks quickly between St. Thomas Hospital and Waggoner's Cycles, which was located in a shopping center to the left of the highway. As we pulled into the lot, a large garage door opened. Ginger parked right in front of the door, and I kept the buffalo gun aimed straight ahead just in case.

"Let's go check it out," I said and exited the Vanguard keeping my helmet on which was still connected to the drones.

A man who looked a whole lot like Derek met us at the door and hurried us inside.

"I know time is tight. I just want to say I appreciate what you've done out there. I have ten bikes ready and waiting. They're fully charged, and they're stocked with ammo and supplies. I wish I could do more."

"You're taking a hundred grand hit by giving us these bikes," Bobby said. "You don't need to do any more. You're the reason we're still in this."

He shook Bobby's hand. "I'm Jack Waggoner. You met my brother Derek. And in a few hours, we'll be proud sponsors."

"I hate to rush, but we're on a timer."

"You do your thing." He stepped back, grinning. "I'm glad we could help. The side cars on the two Taurus are filled with supplies. Food, water, and a few weapons that I scrounged up. I couldn't get enough for everybody, but I got what I could."

"You're a godsend," Larry Southard said as he put one of the helmets on and climbed onto one of the Taurus bikes.

Bolder took the other Taurus. The Tacketts picked a pair of Tornadoes while Munseizer and Polk mounted a pair of Santa Cruzes. Sam and Lila took a Santa Cruz and a Tornado; Tina and Rob picked the two Spiders.

I was a little surprised at the variety, but I suspected these were all used bikes that he had taken in recently as trade-ins. None of them were new but all of them looked to be in fair condition.

I shook the man's hand and returned to the Vanguard.

Waggoner waved as we pulled out of his lot and back onto Medical Center Parkway.

"We have approximately an hour and a half to get as far as we can," I said. "I think we should interlock all the sensors and let me run it through my command control."

"Agreed," Lila said. "You've got that sensor suite and the drones."

"As it gets dark, we can cut our lights and run with the sensors."

"That's putting a lot of faith in that sensor suite of yours," Rob York said. "But it's a damned good sensor suite. Let's do it."

We hit I-24 as the sun dropped below the horizon, my HUD giving me a clear picture of the road ahead of us. We didn't meet anyone as we took the ramp onto I-840.

"All right, let's kick this pig."

"I'll have you know Sascha is not a pig." Ginger punched the throttle, and I was pushed back into my seat.

"Jesus Christ!" Rob exclaimed as we shot ahead of the others. "You weren't kidding. That thing is a rocket on wheels."

The bikes accelerated to catch up.

I concentrated on my HUD as my fingers danced across the control boards. "All sensors calibrated. Sending directly to your HUDs. Cut all lights in ten seconds."

Everyone was seeing the road on their HUDs with clear paths marked in green and obstacles in red. All the lights went out and we shot into the darkness. When Pop taught me how to use the sensors on Charlene, this was how he taught me to do it. Always be aware of the area around you. It worked in life and on the roads.

We passed the Almaville exit at 100 miles an hour and I could see lights in the distance where I suspect would-be raiders were moving toward the highway to set up and intercept us. They didn't appear to be in a hurry, so our secret was still safe. We were quite a few hours earlier than they would've expected us.

"Everything smooth? Sensors are working great, let's put on some more speed."

By the time we passed the Triune exit, we were running 150 miles an hour. The sensors registered more raiders gathering just north of the interstate, but like the previous times, they didn't expect us for hours.

The first time we were actually even seen by anybody was crossing I-65. They still didn't get a chance to set up before we were already gone.

There was little banter among our team as we sped through the night. I suspected they were focused on their HUDs. I remembered my run through Maynardville, using only sensors. I had been doing ninety and it'd been hairy enough.

Two hours of this would be hard on anybody.

Chapter 46

"We're twenty minutes away from our secret being out," I said. "These guys seem to be a whole lot more organized than most of the SOBs we've seen so far."

"Derek said Jackson had been taken over by a mercenary outfit," Southard said. "I was hoping it was an incompetent one."

We clustered around a picnic table. I pointed at my tablet.

"We're not allowed to go around 'em so we need to go through 'em."

The mercs who had taken Jackson didn't leave the road unguarded overnight like the others had. The highway through Jackson was lined with fighting vehicles.

"Back that up." Bobby tapped my arm.

I turned my drone back the way it had come.

"Is that what I think it is?" He asked.

"I think it is," I said.

"I sure as hell don't want to come up against those," Munseizer said.

"Let's steal 'em." Lila was grinning. "I always wanted to run the guns on something like that."

"We have to leave the designated course to get 'em." I pointed where they were parked. "But I think I have a workaround figured out. As long as we bring them back to this point and continue, we're still following the course."

"I think you're right," Polk said. "Let's do it."

I looked back at the tablet at the lot where the two Foster Busnaughts were parked. They looked brand-new and I had no doubt they intended to use those against us. From what I remembered, the Busnaught was a heavily armored behemoth with a lot of weapons. Enough that it took two gunners to run them all. As new as these were they would be the model F, which had a pretty good sensor suite and countermeasures. Unless they had removed them, of course.

"Hell yeah," I said. "I'm tired of just having this one bitty cannon."

"I'm not sure I'll ever ride a motorcycle again," Bobby said. "I'm fairly certain that's the most terrifying thing I've ever done. I definitely want one of those Busnaughts."

"There's nothing sneaky about a Busnaught." I tapped the picture on my tablet.

"That's because you don't have to be sneaky in a Busnaught," he said.

"True enough. Mount up – we don't have long before they can figure where we're at. Let's get those Busnaughts before they do." I climbed back into the Vanguard. "I sure hope those things are full of ammo."

"I reckon if they planned to use them on us, they'll be full," Ginger answered.

"Probably so."

We left the small park and took Highway 412 south toward the old Greyhound bus station. My tablet still listed it as a Greyhound station even though Greyhound had been gone for years. People still traveled in buses when they had to, but they were buses like the two we were about to steal. Armed buses could carry a few passengers but nowhere near what the old Greyhounds used to. Hard to fit people in a bus when you need that space for ammunition.

The road was empty all the way into town. I figured most of them were up by the interstate. My drones showed some activity around the buses as several people were loading them up.

"That's awful nice of 'em," I muttered.

"What?" Ginger asked.

"Looks like their loadin' 'em up for us."

"Then I guess we better take them before they get done and try to use them on us."

"Yup, I reckon so."

We pulled into a wooded area just before the Greyhound station.

"The rest of this is on foot," I said. "Be ready to drive in if we need you, Gin."

"I hate to say it, Jake. But we need you in the gunner chair," Southard said. "If you have to come in with the Vanguard, we're gonna need a gunner in the seat."

He was right. Plus I could spot targets for them with my drones.

"I'll paint targets."

I parked the drones over the Greyhound station as the others made their way through the woodland behind it. There were eight mercs at the bus station. I was pretty sure it was just the crew for the buses. I marked all eight with my HUD and sent it to theirs.

Ginger was running through the Clutch feed, acting like we were preparing to leave the safe zone. We couldn't afford to give away the fact that we'd left yet. We still had about ten minutes before they would know that we had left the room for the garage. The two-hour delay from live to show had been priceless. We didn't have to fire a single shot between Murfreesboro and Jackson. I still had all the ammo that had been dropped at the safe zone by sponsors, and there had been plenty of those. Any excess room in the Vanguard was filled with new ammo boxes.

Taking out the mercenary crews went well except for one small hiccup. One of the guys had gotten off a shot and clipped Polk. It was a flesh wound and he would be fine. I couldn't detect anyone incoming with the drones, so they loaded into the Busnaughts and Lila bandaged his arm.

"It's fully loaded," Bobby said as he slid into the driver seat of one of the buses. "They deserve what's about to happen, considering they were about to use these on us."

Southard started the other bus. "This one's fully loaded, too."

"Let's see if we can get these sensor suites linked up," I said. "It should improve our coverage. We can tie everything through the drones."

"It looks like this one has a pretty good countermeasure suite," Billy said.

"So does this one," York added.

"That's good," I said. "We'll probably need it."

We followed the two buses back up Highway 412 to the interstate. As we rolled onto the interstate the two-hour timer went off.

"Secret's out folks," I said over the com. "They know we're out of the safe zone. Probably another six to eight minutes before they realize we took the bikes. Then a few minutes to figure out how far we could've gotten. We may have ten minutes before they know we could be here."

"Then let's roll right on through," York said. "Right now they think these buses are theirs. Let's use it."

"Agreed," I said. "Let's roll."

"Interstate's got three lanes," Southard said. "Just tuck yourselves right in between us."

"With all of the sensor suites linked," I said, "I'll paint as many targets as I can since we'll be in the middle. I don't have to worry about weapons so I can focus on that. You guys can focus on shootin' stuff."

"Sounds like a plan, boss," Bolder said. "I'm just happy to not be riding a bike. And it's nice to have a bunch of guns this time. Guns and armor, not guns OR armor."

"Amen, brother," Lila said.

Chapter 47

"As you well know folks, this Knoxville pack has been full of surprises! And this is a big one! Who expected them to have a sponsor willing to give them ten motorcycles?"

"That's right, Gavin, they entered that safe zone with one functional vehicle and a Volkswagen minibus. How did they even know about that motorcycle shop? And how did they manage to set it up without the camera seeing?"

"We may have our answer right here, Ellen." Gavin Grey held up a paper. "This is the official sponsorship for every member of the team by Waggoner's Cycles. And they just may have pulled a fast one. Where is our intrepid pack? I think it may be time to do another jump to a live feed!"

"I have to say, Gavin, this Knoxville pack has gone much further than expected and they might just pull this off! Every one of the packs in the Dead Man's Run got off to a bloody start but I'm not sure if any of them rival this one. Although I also have to say the pack in Virginia Beach had to go through a novel way of qualifying for the race. They had to find their vehicles hidden in some quite dangerous places."

"Very true, Ellen. But if anybody could pull that off, it's the Pale Rider!"

"We can't leave a bunch of them behind us," I said. "These things are all about the armor and weapons, but they've got little in the way of speed."

"Then I imagine we should get as close as we can before we announce ourselves," Bobby said.

We were a quarter mile from where the mercs had begun their set up.

"Bobby, I thought you weren't supposed to be here for another couple hours," a voice over the radio in the Busnaught said.

"Thought we'd get here a little early," Bobby answered.

"Hold on a minute. You're not Bobby."

"I beg to differ. I am Bobby, Bobby Tackett at your service."

"Oh shit …" the voice said before the signal cut off.

I had been painting targets since we got the drones within range, and my HUD was peppered with figures outlined in red.

"Fire," I said as we reached firing range.

Most of the crews were outside their vehicles because they didn't expect us for hours. Miniguns fired in short bursts picked off targets as fast as they could switch to the new ones. We didn't even slow down and I continued to paint targets ahead of us.

The overpass in front of us had two armored vans parked atop of the bridge. I marked them both for the antitank guns in the turrets. ATs make short work of enemy vehicles, especially when they're parked right out in the open. I wasn't sure if there was any crew inside of them, but we couldn't take the chance.

"You know what we have here?" Bobby said on the bus's radio. "We have what my hero, Bobby Hank, the Pale Rider, used to call a target-rich environment. And I'm a little bit irate. You see, I sold my favorite Bobby Hank card to get into this stupid race. Twenty-three thousand four hundred and fifty-three dollars is what I got for that card, and we built that Galahad ourselves, only to lose it to a bunch of stupid cannibals. Now I'm still little pissed about that, but we got here and found these lovely buses. Now don't get me wrong, I thank you for giving us these wonderful toys but I'm not sure that we can accept all of it. So, thanks to my fellow participants who agree that we can't keep all of this ammunition, we've decided to give some of it back to you ..."

I chuckled as we cleared the underpass with the burning vans atop.

"We have three trucks incoming from the rear," I said.

Both of the buses dropped mines.

Explosions filled the night as the trucks hit them.

"Plasma mines? Boy, you guys planned to really make a mess out of us, didn't you?" Bobby continued. "Glad we could give those back to you."

"Another overpass ahead, I don't see any vehicles, but there are snipers."

I fired the buffalo gun and turned one of the snipers to a bloody mist. Both buses opened up with the front miniguns, spraying the bridge ahead.

We cleared the second overpass, but there were at least four more of them before we would get out of town. And there was no way they hadn't figured out that we were coming.

"Frack!"

Ginger's exclamation brought me out of my focus on my HUD. "What is it?"

"That son of a bitch went live again!"

I growled as I shook my head. "Nothing to do about it now."

I put my focus back into targeting mercenaries. Gavin Grey was beginning to piss me off. I could hear the show playing in the background.

"Did he just say the Pale Rider? Tell me he didn't just say Pale Rider! Bobby Hank is doing the Dead Man's Run? Holy shit!"

"I don't think that's the takeaway from this, Bobby," Lila said. "Any chance of surprise is now gone."

"Not sure we got to worry about surprise," York replied as a whole line of cars erupted in flames. He had fired the heavy laser from the turret and raked it down the side of the mercs' cars.

"True enough," she said and fired the antitank gun at an armored van.

"At least he did wait until we got started with these guys." I shrugged. "I suppose he could've ruined our surprise and really made a mess."

The bus on our right lurched toward us as something hit the other side with an explosion. Countermeasures had barely caught the rocket before it impacted but the explosion still rocked the bus.

"Stupid rocket!"

"You got a way with words, Bolder."

"I don't need any comments from the peanut gallery, Larry!"

"Then shoot that bastard with the rocket launcher!"

I grinned as the Piranha that had fired the rocket exploded.

The next intersection, Highland Avenue, only had a couple of snipers which we took out handily. But I was a little worried about the next one. According to my drones, there were a lot of vehicles ahead.

262 | P a g e

Chapter 48

"That doesn't look good." The drones picked up a lot of incoming vehicles from the north on 45. "More company. They'll reach the overpass before we do."

"Shit! Why does everything have to be so complicated?" Bobby asked.

"I reckon if it was easy everybody'd be doin' it," I replied.

"How many cars?"

I marked their HUDs.

"Wait a minute. They're shooting each other," I said. "Full speed. Maybe we can get by before there's a winner."

"I swear, the whole world has lost their damn minds," Ginger said, shaking her head as we came within sight of the overpass. We could see the tracers from both sides as they shot at each other.

"Tanks!"

"Where?" Larry asked.

"Both north and south."

"North and south?"

One of the southern tanks fired on one of the northern tanks and they began swapping shots with their main guns.

"Jesus, there's a war going on here and I'm not sure that's about us."

We passed under the bridge, as both armies kept shooting each other. The bridge collapsed shortly after we passed under it.

"Glad they waited long enough for us to get through," Bobby said.

We passed maybe ten vehicles heading the other way that had just gotten onto the interstate from the ramp. They didn't even bother taking a pot shot at us.

"I reckon they have bigger fish to fry," I said.

"What do you think that was all about?" Bobby asked.

"From what I understand," York replied, "the mercs took Jackson just after they announced the course for this race. My guess is the Jackson folks used the distraction of the race to take back their city."

"I wouldn't doubt that," I said. "Our route looks clear for a bit. We probably need to assess our ammo and I can send a drone out ahead of us a ways."

"Since that asshole went live, I don't know how long we have," York said.

"That's a valid point." I sent the number one drone ahead at a faster speed. "Maybe we should keep moving and assess as we go."

"We took some damage on the right side," Larry said. "Probably need to stop for at least a few minutes just to check it out."

"All right, let's pull 'em over for minute. Do a quick check."

"Gotcha, boss."

We pulled over and Larry stepped off to examine the right side of the bus. "Damn, that rocket was a lot closer than I thought. Took a pretty hard hit over here. But there's nothing that affects the driving."

"All right, mount back up and let's roll. Switch sides with the buses so the damaged side is toward the inside."

"Sure thing," Larry said.

"We went through about half of our Vulcan ammo," Lila said. "We can't fire the heavy laser too quickly or it'll take out the power plant. Generators only charge so fast."

"Wonder if we could fit 'em with a second power plant just to fuel the lasers," I replied.

"They have a spot for it, but the generators can only generate so fast. We need to add secondary generators to each axle which gets expensive."

"We make it into Memphis with these things and we'll have a couple of days before we have to head out on the second leg of this race. Mechanics are already there so they can get on it as soon as we arrive."

"I'll call Joe," Bobby said. "He can get ahold of your mechanics and start looking. I want to keep these buses."

"Me too," I said. "It's refreshing to have enough weapons to use."

"We dropped about a third of our mine load back there as well," York said. "As slow as these things are, we need as many mines as we can get."

"True enough." I focused on my lead drone as it started finding targets. "If the Clutch stream is anything to go by, we'll have plenty of cash to buy ammo and weapons. The problem is gonna be getting there. It looks like a rolling fight all the way from Brownsville to the wall. It doesn't look as dense as they were when we came out of Knoxville, but there's gonna be quite a few."

"How the hell did any of those other guys run 1,300 miles?" Bobby asked.

"I've been keeping track," York said. "None of those other packs had designated routes. Hard to set up a trap for somebody you don't know is gonna be there."

"All I can say is I hope we have a better route next time." Bobby eased the bus in alongside of our right side. "This designated route thing sucks."

"How are we on AT ammo, Lila? I'd love to take these guys out at a distance before they ever get close enough."

"We didn't use those much coming through Jackson. How about you Billy? We've almost got a full loadout."

"Same. We've almost got a full load out too."

"Then I'll start paintin' targets. You guys can start shootin' those frackers as soon as they come in range."

"Light 'em up, boss!" Billy yelled and started firing the AT.

The cars were coming straight at us in our lane, which made it easy enough to target them. The biggest problem was their numbers. I wasn't even sure we'd have enough ammunition to shoot them all. We were three quarters of the way through them when we ran out of anti-tank ammo.

"Get close to the front, Gin," I said and opened up with the buffalo gun. "We can take out some of them, so the heavy lasers don't have to use so much power."

She moved just ahead of the two buses where I could use the turret to cover the whole front. We heard the high-pitched whine of the heavy lasers as they raked across the outer edges of the pack of cars heading our way. I focused on the center and put round after round into the lead cars.

As we reached them, we had to drop back and let the buses move the wreckage with their ram plates. We rolled through the gates of Memphis with less than a quarter charge on both power plants. Both buses and the Vanguard were bone dry of ammunition and the interstate was covered in wreckage.

One shot had gotten through into the Vanguard, but it had hit the beer fridge. A piece of shrapnel from the fridge had lodged in my left leg. I shook my head, looking at the twisted door. The thing had saved my life twice despite the shrapnel.

As the gates closed behind us it was like stepping into a completely different world with cheering crowds lining the streets.

"The world has gone completely nuts," Ginger said quietly.

"That it has," I said, looking down at the jagged piece of metal sticking out of my leg. "We need to get to the med center."

She looked back at me. "Jesus, Jake!"

"It's okay, Gin, it's not going anywhere."

"Anyone else injured?" She asked over the com.

"Polk could still use some help. I patched him up, but it could stand to be looked at."

"Both the Tacketts took a little shrapnel," Tina said. "I took over the driving just before we reached the gate."

"Then we go straight to the med center," Ginger said.

Chapter 49

"It looks like the Jacksonites have taken back Jackson, Ellen."

"That's right, Gavin. They used the race as a distraction to get their forces close enough. I think they planned to have Jackson back under their control before the Knoxville pack even arrived. Due to their quick travel, our intrepid racers made it much easier for the Jacksonites."

"No doubt about that, Ellen."

"I don't think anyone expected any of this pack from Knoxville to actually make it through the initial gauntlet that was the first leg of the Dead Man's Run. I'm certain they didn't expect half of them to make it."

"There've been rumors of multiple teams ready to run from Memphis to continue the Dead Man's Run, because of course there can't be a race without racers. I wonder if it's true, and I wonder if they planned to add teams to the Knoxville pack until they're back up to twelve."

"It's possible, of course. But who knows?"

"I have to say, Gavin, I am quite impressed with the way this Knoxville pack is working together now."

"Me too, Ellen. And the addition of the Foster Busnaughts is quite the game changer."

"That is a fact, Gavin. Those two buses have more firepower then all the Knoxville cars combined."

"Oh my," Gavin said. "It looks like there are some more shenanigans going on, but I have been chastised for going live. You're just going to have to wait a couple hours to see it, viewers. This pack has been very interesting to say the least."

The nurse was just finishing the bandage on my leg when Billy pushed open the curtain, dragging someone else.

"Boss, we got a problem. This guy just said they have some guy named Dirk set up to take out our guys as they go into Gold Cross."

I was on my feet almost too quick for the nurse to get out of the way.

"Where is he?"

"You don't think I'm telling you anything, do ya?"

I snatched the man completely off his feet, slammed him onto the bed I had been laying on, and planted the nurse's scalpel into his right leg.

"You'll tell me everything."

Billy, Bobby, and I limped up the stairs to the massive Gold Cross facility. Ginger was sitting inside in one of the chairs in the lobby with Lila and Sam.

"It's hard to believe we were running for our lives twelve hours ago," Lila said.

"Inside the city walls is completely different," Sam said and pointed. "Although it's got its own weird shit. Some dude jumped off of a high-rise, just over there."

"Where did you get that?" Ginger asked pointing at the sniper rifle strapped across my back. "That's new, isn't it?"

"New donor," I said.

Bobby snorted.

"What?" She asked. "Never mind, I probably don't want to know."

"We're ready for you, ladies," a tech said as she opened the door and looked out. "You gentlemen need to register at the desk."

I nodded and the three of us went to the desk.

We were on our respective machines in about thirty minutes. I let my mind wander for a while as the computer did what it did. It took about two hours to do an upload. The guy, Dirk, had been exactly where the other fellow had told me, and the rifle was very nice. Wasn't sure what I would do with the Barrett, but it was a very nice gun, and I didn't want to leave it laying on the rooftop.

I hoped that Pop would make it to Memphis before we drove out. I wanted to thank him and Charlie for going out on a ledge for us. And I definitely owed Flatford.

According to what we'd already been told, our challenge would be starting up early in the morning. I wondered what kind of stupid shit they would have lined up for us.

The table slid out of the machine, and I sat up. At least, if nothing else, new me would know what happened up to this point. Even with all the shit that happened I didn't want to forget it. I picked the Barrett up as I left the room and slung it over my shoulder by the strap.

Ginger was waiting in the lobby as I exited the hallway. She pointed at the television on the wall with the scene frozen on the screen.

"You threw a guy off a roof?"

I shrugged. "Unreasonable people make life difficult."

"Who was he aiming the gun at?"

"Not sure," I said. "But his cohort at the hospital seemed to think he was planning to take you guys out as you went into Gold Cross today. I figured I would ask him nicely."

"That was asking nicely?"

I shrugged again. "Nice as he was gonna get."

I heard a snicker behind me.

"Dude deserved it," Billy said. "They were bent out of shape after our run into the city. Guess they were looking forward to catching us on motorcycles instead of buses."

She shook her head with one eyebrow raised, stepped forward, and locked her arm in mine. "Let's go see Jackie."

Chapter 50

My hand was halfway to my hand cannon before I realized the grease covered projectile was Jackie Shoffner. I caught her midair and her arms wrapped around my neck.

"I knew you could make it!"

She dropped to the floor and ran to Ginger.

"You two scared the shit out of me."

"Me too," Ginger said.

Billy was standing next to Ginger with a big grin on his face.

Jackie laughed and hugged him too.

"Forsaken for a hot chick," Joe Tackett commented as he strode up to his brothers.

He engulfed Billy and Bobby both in his huge arms. "Thought I lost you there for a minute."

Ginger and Jackie backed away from us whispering and Joe turned to me.

"You, my friend, are one crazy son o' ma bitch. But I can't thank you enough for bringing these two dumb asses back with you."

"They fought their way across this damn state. All I did was give 'em the chance."

The other two brothers were walking around the Busnaught Joe had been working on.

"I looked into you a bit. You didn't go there to fight a bunch of cannibals. I'm thinking you went there to keep them from being tortured. And that's a whole other thing. By all rights it would've been the right call. Somewhere along the way, you decided not to."

I was glad my plan had changed when I reached the Speedway. I wasn't sure exactly where it changed. I think it might've been when I realize the girls were being kept in a different place. Maybe it was before that. I wasn't sure.

"I don't know where exactly it happened."

"Just know that I'm glad it did. The three of us are all we have left."

"This thing ain't over," I said.

"But right now we're still here and not one of those corporate bastards expected us to be."

"You're right, there."

"I reckon I need to get back to it," he said. "We got another day and a half to get everything we can repaired or installed on these buses. We got six sets of drones to add to your net during overwatch, three sets on each bus. You'll have fifteen drones at your disposal routed through the Vanguard.

"Fifteen?" I stopped in my tracks. "How do we even afford that?"

"You haven't been payin' attention to the Clutch stream, have you?"

"Not really. It's more Ginger's thing. I hate it."

He laughed. "You've had close to eighty thousand dollars sent to your account through the stream."

"Holy shit!"

"No one's even touched that. The drone system was donated through various sponsors. You give Jackie and me the okay and we'll tap that too."

I waved toward Jackie who walked back toward me with a huge smile on her face.

"How do I give you authority to access my account from the Clutch stream?"

"You already have an authorization form. Just sign it." She grinned evilly. "Are you sure you want to do that? I might take all that cash, grab up one of these girls and run off."

I shrugged. "It would probably serve me right."

"You like girls?" Joe asked. "Billy will be heartbroken. He was smitten the second he saw you running toward them covered in grease."

"She's left a trail of heartbroken men along the way, Joe," I said. "Reckon Billy will get over it in a few years."

"Just a few years?" Jackie's left eyebrow raised.

"He hasn't seen you run around in your skivvies. That one takes decades."

She giggled and handed me her tablet. "Sign that and we'll get to work."

I looked at the screen and amazement at the number there. "Is that right?"

"Yup." Jackie pointed at the cameras at the other end of the garage that were kept out of the grease pit. "Seems you got pretty popular after chopping up a bunch folks with an ax."

"They were all bad folks."

"Yes, they were."

As soon as I signed the tablet, she started pressing buttons. The tablet pinged repeatedly as order after order went through.

"I had everything already set up. Sascha is about to get an upgrade."

"She got you calling it Sascha too?"

"That's her name."

"All right, whatever. I need a new beer fridge."

"Really?"

"Damn thing saved my life twice and the shine's better when it's cold."

"You don't need to be drinking out there anyway."

"You don't think I'm gonna do this sober, do you?"

"All right already." She pressed another button on the tablet to another ping. "Beer fridge."

"I want some extra armor around the front."

"That was already in the plan."

"Good," I said.

"I don't need to ask why you want that," she said glancing over at Ginger. "I don't sense any of the animosity there was before."

"I'm still not sure what's happening. She saw it all and didn't run."

"Jesus Christ, Jake, the whole damn country saw it and you went from the bottom of the ratings to the top. Deep blue hero shit."

"Not a hero." I shook my head and walked toward Ginger. "A hero wouldn't have enjoyed it."

Chapter 51

"Pyramid full of cannibals?" Lila muttered from my left. "What the Frak?"

"I think Pop told me about that place," I said. "They use it as a prison. You commit the crime, they send you in the front. If you make it out the back, your sentence is served."

Since we were a day ahead of the other team that was coming to Memphis, we would have the option of choosing which challenge to face.

"I don't know about the rest of you," she retorted. "I think I've had enough of cannibals."

"Ditto."

"Agreed."

Everyone seemed to be in agreement, so it was easy enough to choose "Gary's Gauntlet" instead. The challenge itself was pretty vague.

"Well, I mean, do we get to throw Jake in there with an axe for a half hour or so?" Oscar asked.

"I'd rather not do that again … ever."

He held both hands up in surrender. "Just checking."

I chuckled.

Ginger squeezed my hand under the table.

"Well since we can't do that, my vote is Gary's Gauntlet, whatever that is." Oscar stood up favoring his shoulder. "I guess we just need to step back out there on the stage and give them the verdict."

"True enough," Bobby said and stood as well. "Who's the front man?"

"Right now Jake's leading in the ratings," Southard said.

"Put me in front of the speaker and that'll end."

"He's right about that. The crowd doesn't respond well to a grumpy bastard," Ginger said with a nod.

"He'd probably just tell everybody to frack off," Sam said as she and Lila stood. "Next is Ginger, then me in the ratings. She'd be a better choice. My rating didn't really climb until my boobs came out. I probably shouldn't do that up on stage."

"Heh," I grunted. "Reckon I can stand there behind her."

"Just try not to look like you're going to kill anyone," Bobby said.

"That's kind of hard with this stupid shirt on."

"What's wrong with the shirts?" Bobby asked. "I picked them up as soon as I saw them."

"You just got them backwards." I pointed toward Ginger's shirt. "She's the Killbilly."

"I'm pretty sure there's no way that you can convince anyone that you're the hometown honey, Jake," Rob York said.

Tina Maples laughed. "Yeah, that ship's sailed."

I looked at Sam. "Starts getting too bad, you can always let the puppies out."

She grinned. "I'll keep 'em loaded and ready."

Ginger elbowed me in the rib.

"I bet if you flashed yours, you'd be in the lead again, Ginger." Lila giggled. "Of course, it might damage that hometown honey image."

"What do you think our intrepid car warriors will decide, Gavin?"

"To be honest Ellen, I doubt they're going to go for the cannibals a second time. Which probably doesn't bode well for the team out of Virginia Beach. They'll be stuck with the 'Cannibal Pyramid' when they get here."

"It looks like our team is returning to the stage! That didn't take very long, Gavin. It appears they've decided to put the Hometown Honey in front of the microphone, and I think that's probably a very good choice. She's been very high in the ratings from the moment she started using the Clutch stream."

"Absolutely. And that's what this is when it boils down to the core of it. It's a ratings game. The only other member of the team from Knoxville with a higher rating is her gunner, Jake Turner. But I have strong doubts that it's because of his interaction with fans." Gavin laughed. "The man was scary before this race began, and he is absolutely terrifying, now."

"I have my doubts that any of the cannibals from the Nashville Speedway are fans."

"Very true. I understand the majority of them are still headed north."

"Indeed! And I can't really blame them, Gavin. Can you?"

"Nope. I'd be driving north until there weren't any more roads."

"I have to say I like the way this group of drivers and gunners have closed ranks and become one team. It's not what we see from most of the other packs. And we might not have seen it in this one if not for the fact that they were all pushed together when they lost most of their vehicles."

"I disagree, Ellen. From the moment they left Knoxville this team stuck right together. If you remember, there were only two of them that weren't in that initial cluster, and they were destroyed fairly quickly. I think someone in that pack was working behind the scenes to get everyone to work together."

"That might be, Gavin. It almost fell apart at the Nashville Speedway. Three teams continued on to Murfreesboro while two stopped."

"And all three of those teams would've been out of the race. Instead one of them was brought back into the pack at Murfreesboro. Sadly, the other two didn't survive."

"I'm not sure who has been keeping everything organized since then, but I have a feeling it might just be Jake Turner. I might not have thought so until we found out his grandfather is none other than Jeremy Hood. Or at least one iteration of the man. Hood was a savant when it came to running multiple guns and multiple targets."

"I believe you're probably right, Ellen. The whole pack seems to move together, and they have been particularly devastating. I watched the replay of their run into the city with those buses. There was no overlapping of targets and that has Hood written all over it."

"Here comes the verdict. Will they face cannibals again or risk the mystery gauntlet?"

The crowd and the huge auditorium went wild as Ginger stepped up to the microphone. She was grinning from ear to ear and waving at everybody. She was very good at this part. Me? Not so much.

I glanced behind us at the two huge screens that were covered by huge golden doors. One of them said "Pyramid" and the other said "Gary's Gauntlet."

"Hi everybody," she said.

The crowd cheered again.

"Miss Yates, I gather your team has decided on the challenge?"

"Yes sir," Ginger answered.

"So what will it be? The Pyramid? Or Gary's Gauntlet?"

"Well, I think we've had about all the cannibals we can stand, so we've unanimously decided that we'll be doing the Gary's Gauntlet challenge."

The host of the show turned to look at us and we all nodded.

"Gary's Gauntlet it is!" He yelled. "Bailey, please show them what they'll be facing!"

A beautiful blonde in a minuscule bikini strutted across the stage to push a button beside the second door. It slid to the side to reveal an aerial view of an immense quarry. McKeller Park was printed in capital letters above the image.

"As most locals know, McKeller Park was purchased in 2025 and turned into a quarry. In the thirty years after that, it was a popular supplier of rock to the whole area. They were the primary supplier when the city walls were built. It was sold to the Tennessee Titan Authority twelve years ago. When they began planning this event, Gary Bolgeo, himself, began to design what we call Gary's Gauntlet. As you can see, the quarry is very similar in shape to a popular arena in Texas that many of you would be aware of. The Double Drum has been a popular arena since its inception.

Our car warriors will be tasked with entering the first drum and following the roads all the way down to the bottom. As you can see, there are some harrowing turns. When they reached the bottom, they will have to traverse the tunnel to the other side and make their way back to the top."

I was studying the aerial photo. What he described wasn't all that complicated, but I knew better. The other shoe was yet to drop.

"Now we don't call it the gauntlet for nothing," he said. "There are various obstacles along the way, including each other. The road dropping to the floor of the quarry is only wide enough for one vehicle. The floor of the quarry is littered with obstacles such as berms, pits, and the biggest obstacle of all. Let's hear a Memphis welcome to the Red Skulls!"

My left eye began to twitch as the door opened across the stage and two men strode out wearing black leather with spikes. Their faces were painted red with black around the eyes to look like skulls. I didn't follow autoduelling, and I still recognized them.

"I'm beginning to remember cannibals fondly," Bobby said from beside me.

"Me too," I muttered.

"All right, car warriors! Are… You… Ready?"

The crowd went crazy again and one of the Red Skulls made rude gestures toward Ginger with his tongue. "I've got something for you, girly."

She reached into her pocket. "Well I got something for you too."

Pulling her hand from her pocket, she gave him the finger.

The Red Skull stepped toward her and, in less than a second, my hand cannon pointed between his eyes.

"You want to start this early?" I asked.

His eyes widened and he halted. Recovering his composure, he smirked and stepped back. "I'm going to enjoy this."

"Not as much as you think."

Bobby snorted from behind me.

284 | P a g e

Chapter 52

I punched buttons on my tablet. Three drones rose from the top of the Vanguard and shot off into the night.

"Where you sendin' those?" Ginger asked as she stepped up beside me.

"They'll be up there with the news drones. Figured we could use every advantage we can get. They can be tied in with everyone's helmets to give them a HUD of the whole quarry."

"Are you allowed to use those?"

"There's no rule forbidding it."

"Well you're not allowed to use drones in the arena."

"Official arenas are designated by the AADA. I looked at the registered list of AADA sanctioned arenas and this isn't on 'em. Nothing in the rules they gave me for this gauntlet say anything about it."

I pointed toward the tablet at the rules of engagement. "Only turrets can fire on us as we descend along the wall. The road makes three laps around the outer wall before it reaches the bottom plus this hairpin on the last leg of the road. The Skulls will be in the tunnel, and they are allowed to open fire on us as soon as we hit the bottom of the pit."

"So if we do it right, we can probably take out those turrets on the way down so all we have to deal with is the Skulls when we hit the bottom." She paused. "Which depends on how many turrets they have and where they're located."

"If that's the only weapon they have that can fire on us on the way down then they have to be within range of our weapons."

"Unless they're rocket turrets."

"Bite your tongue, woman."

She laughed.

It had been too long since I'd heard that. And it was nice to hear even amidst all the death and destruction that surrounded us. I put my tablet on the table and sat down in one of the chairs in what we called the drivers' lounge. The garage where the work was being done on our vehicles and the adjoining rooms were off-limits to the cameras. No one was actually allowed to see our builds before we exited the city on the second leg of the Dead Man's Run.

Ginger dropped into my lap with her legs hanging over the arm of the chair. "What do you think they're going to do on the second leg?"

"I reckon they're gonna try to kill us like they did on the first leg. This time we don't have Flatford and his truck to lead the way. But we do have two Busnaughts."

"If Jackie and Joe have anything to do with it, the damn things will be indestructible," she said. She looked around the room with a grin and wiggled in my lap. "You know the cameras can't see in here and we have a couple hours before we leave for the challenge."

"Say no more," I said and pulled her in close. "What if one of them comes in the door?"

She reached into her pocket. "Then I got something for them too."

I laughed and stood up with her in my arms. We moved toward the couch as various articles of clothing dropped on the floor and, for just a little while, I didn't feel like a monster.

"A Flamberge?" Ginger shook her head. "Not gonna be a lot of room inside of it."

Rothschild had built the Flamberge for the highway. It was a pretty popular car on the roads because it was affordable. Which was probably the reason they were provided for this challenge. Cost-efficient had always been important to the TTA. It had been like pulling teeth to get new equipment for the road crews when I worked for them.

"At least we won't lose any of the standard load because they put in a gunner's chair." Bobby looked inside car number two. "These come with gunner stations." He straightened up. "At least it's the turret model. Those miniguns can fire in any direction."

"I like turrets," I said.

"I like front guns." Tina was looking at the recoilless rifles on the front of the third Flamberge. "Typically front guns trigger from the steering wheel."

"You're just mad when you don't get to shoot something," York, her gunner, said.

"Maybe."

Oscar Polk pointed at the back of their car. "Rear mounted rockets."

I open the door and slid into the gunner seat to cycle through the weapon system. I poked my head out the window. "Guided rockets."

"Sweet!" Billy Tackett rubbed his hands together.

"Too bad we don't have any way to target them past our car sensors," York said.

"Put your helmet on," I said with a grin.

He placed the helmet on his head and his coms went live. "Oh you devious bastard."

Billy and Lila both put their helmets on followed quickly by Bolder and Polk.

"You can't use drones in arenas." Lila sounded worried.

Before I could answer, York had already figured it out. "AADA registered arenas. I'm guessing this one isn't on the register."

"Yep."

"That's skating awful close to the edge there, Turner."

"We've been on the edge from the beginning of this thing. I didn't see any reason to change it now."

"True enough," Bolder agreed. "If they want us to follow the rules, they need to follow them too."

"I can't fault you there," Billy said and climbed into the gunner seat of the second Flamberge. "Let's kick this pig."

Chapter 53

I triggered the display in everyone's HUD as we pulled out of the enclosed garage where we got to see our cars for the first time. Outside were thousands of people lined up on both sides of a 30-foot alley that led to the entrance to the quarry.

The aerial photo we had seen in the introduction did little to reveal what was on the other side, but my drones were already up with the news drones above the quarry, and we were receiving real-time footage. I began designating targets throughout the quarry where obvious turrets were placed. There were six of them close to the outside walls that circled the quarry in a long oval. As we circled the walls there would be at least three turrets able to fire at us in any given position. Luckily, they could only fire at one car at a time and there were six of us.

"Are you ready for this?" I asked.

"Hell yeah!"

Ginger hit the throttle and we shot through the entrance faster than I expect they anticipated. We knew exactly what was on the other side of the thick wall, though. The wall was there to prevent random gunfire escaping the quarry. The road we were on turned into a tunnel to the right which led into the first quarry. I almost expected a surprise turret to pop up, but I guess they already had enough inside the quarry.

As we exited the tunnel she took a sharp right. Ahead of us was the ramp leading around the quarry three times at a five percent grade. The road had about two feet on each side of the car, and I was quite happy that Ginger was driving and not me.

I spun the miniguns to the left and dropped their elevation. The first turret opened fire at the same time I did, and bullets peppered the side of the Flamberge. We were in range of three turrets at the same time for just a moment before Bobby reached the range of the first one and it swung to him.

"They're set to target the closest car," I said.

"That's actually better for us," Billy said as he opened fire on the first turret.

I was still firing on the same turret as he was. The other two were closer ranged but we could focus on one where the programming would spread out their fire. Fire erupted from the turret, and it stopped shooting.

"One down!" Billy yelled and started firing at the second turret.

We rounded the end of the oval and I targeted the same turret as Billy. I lost the target as we passed a certain point in the oval and switched to the closest one on the wall behind us. Our front guns were fairly useless for this and the miniguns were about the only thing we could use unless I wanted to fire one of the rockets. It would silence them that much quicker, but I had a feeling we would need them when we went up against the Red Skulls. We still didn't know what they would be driving.

York opened fire as soon as he came within range of the one Billy had been targeting. He must've gotten a good hit because with the drones I could see smoke coming from the top of it and it stopped shooting.

Meanwhile we were taking fire from three turrets along the wall underneath the initial ramp coming into the quarry. We were almost back to where we entered the quarry when Munseizer and Polk entered. We had dropped 50 feet or so.

There were six cars now circling the pit and the turret fire was noticeably less per car. I could take a moment to study the floor of the "arena." There were some walls that would block gunfire in various positions, which could be helpful. But it would keep it from concentrating our fire on any one point, which was more advantageous for a single target than six targets.

"Only one shootin' at us this round," I said and immediately regretted it when three more turrets popped up on top of the artificial walls. These could target anywhere around them. "Frack!"

Incoming fire increased, but the turrets were still set to fire on the closest targets, so they kept switching between our cars as we moved around them.

"I guess six wasn't enough," Billy said over the com.

I lit up one of the middle turrets with my HUD.

"On it," York said

All six cars opened fire on the single turret. It exploded in seconds, and we switched. This time I had lit up both of them and sent three to Billy, Lila, and York. The other turret was targeted by me, Bolder, and Polk. It took a few seconds more before both of them went inactive. There was one more turret on the opposite wall and I targeted it, leaving everyone to pick their own targets as they descended the far wall.

We rounded the end of the oval again with only two turrets remaining. There was a lot of damage on the driver sides of all of our cars though. The bullet-resistant glass cracked just before the last turret went down.

"That was close," Ginger said. "At least if we have to climb the other side with turrets firing, they'll be firing on the passenger side."

"True."

The last trip around the quarry on the lowest ramp was ominously quiet.

"What do you think they'll be driving?"

"Somethin' nasty." I was fairly certain it was going to be bad.

"Probably so. We'll know soon enough. We're almost to the bottom." She ducked and looked around the ledges in front of us. "If we hadn't killed all the turrets on the way down this little turn up ahead would be a beast. Have to almost come to a stop."

"Keep your head on a swivel. It's just the sort of place they'd lay a trap." I scanned the area. "I almost think that's what the pop-up turrets were for. I don't think they expected us to take the other turrets out as quickly. All three of those have a firing solution on this point."

"You're probably right," she said as she turned the hairpin and started down the last ramp. She slowed is we neared the bottom to let the others get closer. "Are you ready for this?"

I pulled the flask from my pocket and took a big swig. "I reckon."

Straight from the bottom of the ramp about 100 feet out was what they called a pit. It was crystal clear water that according to my drone sensors was well over 100 feet deep. To the right was a 25-foot wall of reinforced brick and concrete. There were two paths we could take straight forward, then to the right, away from the pit, or circle around the pit and around another 25-foot wall to head back up the far side.

"Right?" she asked.

"Up to you. We'll have a clear shot of the tunnel mouth."

She hit the throttle, and we hit the bottom of the ramp.

My drones were focused on the mouth of the tunnel. The Red Skulls came barreling out as soon as our wheels touched the bottom of the pit.

"Frack! What is it with these pricks and fire?"

Chapter 54

"I have to say this group from Knoxville has been just full of surprises, Ellen."

"You're right there, Gavin. There was a little rush inspection of the rules when the judges realized they were using drones."

"The funny thing is this team did the research. Going by the guidelines set down before them for this match, it's perfectly legal."

"They still took a pounding going down the ramp by those turrets."

"Ellen, we're about to find out what all the mystery's been about with the Red Skulls. Everyone's been very tightlipped about what they'd be driving … And the racers have reached the bottom!"

"Is that a tank?"

"Not a tank, Ellen, but in regard to those vehicles down there it might as well be. It has a distinctly military air about it with all that armor."

"Well, Gavin, it doesn't seem to be deterring our team from Knoxville! Ginger Yates didn't even slow down … That's a flamethrower, isn't it? Definitely a flamethrower."

"I don't think we could even scratch the paint on that thing," I said.

Ginger went full throttle. "Best thing we can do is to outrun it."

"Left side, everyone!"

My coms clicked as they all acknowledged.

"Full throttle! We need to get into that tunnel where they can't shoot us."

"Yeah, but what then?" Billy asked.

"I have a plan if we can reach the tunnel."

My fingers worked furiously at the controls as I plotted a scenario.

"Jesus, Jake." Bobby said. "Will it work?"

"If there's enough of us, it might."

The armored behemoth in front of us opened fire with miniguns. My turret was shredded. I could see smoke and fire with my drones, and I lost sensors for the miniguns.

"Frack!"

Fire rolled across our Flamberge as we passed on the left side of the Skulls. If we'd been on the other side, it probably would've gotten in because of the damaged armor. As it was it was very close. We shot past them and made for the tunnel. Everyone followed suit with various amounts of damage.

The Skulls slammed on brakes and turned. Thankfully the behemoth took a minute to turn around. We were all in the tunnel except for Munseizer and Polk. Their Flamberge took a rocket directly to the power plant. Flame erupted from the inside, and I winced. The coms were still live and the screams from inside the car as the Skulls stopped to flood their car with the flamethrower told us everything we needed to know.

We were all silent as the screams abruptly ended.

One by one the targeting systems were slaved to my console, and I input target coordinates for every rocket we had.

"Full stop, Gin."

We stopped about a hundred and fifty feet in front of the tunnel.

With my sensors I could see the Skulls tearing through the tunnel. Even as turrets began pouring gunfire into our vehicles from this side of the tunnel, I kept my focus until the Skulls were a hundred and fifty feet from the end of the tunnel.

I triggered twenty rockets, four from each car. Ginger accelerated and I watched the sensors. My miniguns were dead and the only thing we had was the front guns. Hopefully the others could take out the turrets.

The rule stated that we can't attack our opponent while they were in the tunnel. It didn't say anything about shooting rocks.

The rockets impacted about 20 feet above the tunnel mouth, and everything seemed to move in slow motion as all the rock gave way. The Skulls were still 50 feet in when the tunnel came down.

"That's gonna leave a mark!" Bobby yelled.

"Hopefully the road's still good enough to get out," I said.

The Tacketts' power plant went down just past the first wall where they were under fire from a turret. It just kept firing at them since they were the closest. I could see both of them burrowing down in the seats as Ginger flew past, straight toward the turret which began firing at us. Not for long, though. She sent the car into a slide and the rear fender slammed into the turret with a crunch. Sparks flew and the gun stopped firing.

She throttled again and with a screech of metal pulled away from the mangled turret dragging the back of the car. There were three turrets left and none of us had any weapons, but Ginger's strategy worked quite well. The other three cars took out the other three turrets in a similar fashion.

"We don't have any cars left," Ginger said.

"No one's shootin' at us either," I said and opened my door. "They said we needed to come out the other side. They didn't say anything about the cars coming out the other side.

Ten of us walked out the tunnel at the top of the second quarry. I sent one of my drones down into the other end of the tunnel and it hit a solid cave-in just over halfway through. I suspected the next time we saw the Red Skulls would be in a new set of bodies.

None of us said much as we walked out. There were crowds of people as far as I could see. A van drove toward us through the crowd. They stopped in front of us so we could get in.

"Need a ride, kid?"

"Hey, Pop."

I climbed in after everyone else.

"This is just crazy." Bobby Tackett looked like he was vibrating. "I'm riding in the car with the freaking Hoods."

"You should've brought your trading cards," Billy said. "You could get them signed."

"Son o' ma bitch! I guess it's out of the question to run back to Knoxville?"

There was a thunk as someone smacked the back of his head.

"Just wonderin'. You don't have to get violent about it."

I grinned and pulled the flask from my pocket. I took a long drink and laid my head back as Ginger nestled into my side.

Chapter 55

I sipped coffee, leaning against the doorway to the bedroom where Ginger lay sprawled across the bed. She had always been a bed hog. I stepped out and eased the door closed.

If we didn't have two more legs of this stupid race looming over our heads, I could almost feel happy ... if I didn't think too hard about all the things I'd done. It was always at the back of my mind, though.

There was a light knock at the door. I found Pop standing outside when I opened it. His arm was in a sling which I hadn't noticed yesterday as I climbed into the van.

I pointed toward it. "Were you wearin' that yesterday?"

"No. Couldn't let that flock of vultures know that Jeremy Hood ain't immortal."

"Have I told you how much I hate this racket?"

"A few times. I used to enjoy it. Kept my identity a secret for a reason, didn't want a bunch of reporters and all this crazy shit showin' up at the farm."

He stepped forward and wrapped his left arm around me. "God, I thought I lost you, boy."

"I thought so, too, Pop."

As he stepped by me into the room, he pointed at the coffee cup. "That's an improvement."

"Just the first cup, Pop."

"Still ... Wasn't that long ago you were startin' the morning with a pint of liquor."

"Thought I might give it till at least 10 o'clock."

He chuckled. "I noticed there's only one suite. You two managed to get that all worked out."

"I reckon everybody in the country noticed." I pointed toward the tablet on the coffee table. "She was answering questions on the Clutch feed for at least three hours last night."

"The group from Virginia Beach should be getting here sometime today. Then the countdown begins. You'll have a day before having to head out again."

"Yeah, they're supposed to give us our next route tomorrow mornin' if everything goes as planned."

"Tonight they have you scheduled for a show with that asshole, Gavin Grey."

"He's not that bad."

"Going live in the middle that Speedway thing was uncalled for."

"He waited until I was about to lose my surprise anyway." I sat down in the chair and motioned toward the sofa. "He could've really screwed things up if he'd gone earlier."

"I guess."

"He went for the highest ratings. Would you expect any better of them?"

"Wasn't this bad when I was wearing the hood."

"Been doing a little reading about Jeremy Hood," I said. "You know it was gettin' a lot worse right before you quit."

"True enough," he grumbled. "Doesn't mean I have to like it."

I nodded and sipped my coffee.

There was another knock on the door.

"Charlie?"

"She's across town."

I stood and walked to the door. When I opened it, there was a very large man in a suit standing there.

"Mister Bolgeo would like to have a word, Mister Turner."

"You don't say?" I shrugged and stepped backward to open the door all the way.

The large man stepped inside the room. He was built like a linebacker for a deathball team. After he surveyed the room a second man stepped in. He was of medium build and his suit was probably worth more than our Vanguard. His hair was jet black and he sported a stylish beard and mustache. It was hard not to recognize the man who was the CEO of Tennessee Titan Authority, Gary Bolgeo.

"Mister Turner," he said, extending a hand. "It's very good to meet you in person."

There was a slight tick in my left eye as I shook his hand. "I haven't quite decided if it's good to meet you or not. It seems you've been trying your level best to kill me for the last three days."

"Rest assured, if I wanted you dead, you'd be dead. This race, this whole event, is about more than you could possibly know. Your story alone has been great for the ratings. Throw in the story of your girl and a tragic romance and you have ratings gold."

"I don't give one damn about the ratings," I said.

"I know that, and it makes you even more popular with the viewers. Insane, isn't it?"

"I guess." I shrugged. "So what has the CEO of the TTA visitin' me at the crack of dawn?"

"Right to the point. I do like that about you. You're straightforward." He took a long breath. "You see, there's a lot of money being wagered on every aspect of this race. A lot more even in the background that no one sees. One of these wagers has become a problem."

"The hell has that got to do with me?"

"It doesn't, yet."

"Okay?"

"In the broader world of corporations, we've never really been considered an equal. We are part of the lawless lands, and thus not the equal of the 'lawful' corporations.

"They can't accept that we had the temerity to sponsor our own team for this and they stepped forward to slap us down. Every one of them had put bounties on their own drivers to make the race more dangerous. I refused to do so and one of them hired mercenaries who attacked my friends' home in Tunica. They killed seven guards, three maids, and took my daughter hostage. They send me live videos every so often to show they haven't hurt her. But that only lasts as long as I toe the line and follow their company line."

"The bounties on the racers."

"Yes. They came directly from me. Now you know the reason why. They can't have us upstarts showing them up. Your success has made that even worse for them. No one expected any of you to make it as far as Crossville. All that happened afterward just cemented you in the hearts and minds of fans across the country."

"And that put your daughter in even more danger."

"Yes, it does."

"What exactly are you here to ask me?"

Chapter 56

"That's the crux of it," I said leaning over the map.

"And the bounties?"

"Removed. He can't guarantee that other corporations won't put bounties on our heads, but his will be lifted, and we'll have one hell of a sponsor."

"Gary frackin Bolgeo." Bobby looked dazed.

"Part of the set-up of this whole thing was that they would send the second team from Memphis, when we didn't make it, to take over and finish the race. It's disguised in the clauses on the contracts. They planned for a twelve team replacement. Now they replaced seven teams, so we'll have some more teams joining us later today. Our route is west through Little Rock, where we'll do a small job for the Bolgeos. Once that's done, successfully I might add, the bounties are lifted officially and Bolgeo is behind us all the way."

"We're drivers and gunners, not infiltration experts."

"That's where the new teams come in. They *are* infiltration experts, and we need to make sure they make it to Little Rock. The thing is we can't talk about this once we are out in public where the cameras can see. But this rescue needs to be on live television so that they can't kill her. We have all the information, so we need to make the plan before we step out of this room. Is everyone in?"

"Boss, you waded through a field of cannibals for us," Bobby said in one of his rare serious tones. "You say we do this, I'm in."

Billy nodded.

"Same here. Things were just about to get real ugly when you stepped in there," Sam said.

"Damn straight," Lila agreed.

"Why the hell not?" Bolder asked. "Hell, Larry'll get lost, and we'd end up there anyway."

"That only happened the one time."

I grinned.

"I'm surprised you didn't try to negotiate for your girl's Gold Cross." York took a drink from the beer in front of him and motioned toward Ginger with the bottle

"I did try. He can't let us go now, we're too popular. The best he can do is throw his complete backing behind us."

He nodded and looked at Tina. "Let's do it."

"Munseizer's not here to say it, so I will. We're all fracking crazy. When do we meet this team of specialists?"

Ginger squeezed my hand.

"When we leave this room and meet 'em, they're just seven more teams of racers."

"Then I guess what we need to do is work up a plan to keep them alive." York leaned forward to look at the map. "I doubt it's going to be as bad as the run out of Knoxville to Crossville, but there's still going to be a lot of people waiting for us. I expect Forrest City and Brinkley to be problem spots."

"Then let's figure out some defensive tactics," Billy said. "Hard to slide seven cars inside the formation and still keep up the appearance for the public."

"And that's the job laid out in front of us."

"Let's get to work," Southard said.

I stepped out of the garage into the sunlight to find a group of cars parked out front.

"Reckon they could of gotten a little bit more original," I muttered.

There were two Rockwell station wagons armed a lot like the one the Sevierville Slammers, Tina and York, started the race with. A Dragon was parked next to them and another at the far end of the line. One of the remaining three was a Bombardier. The other two I wasn't familiar with, but I would look them up.

One of the members of the first team walked up to me. "Pleasure to meet you, Turner. You've done a hell of a job."

"Welcome." I shook his hand.

"Name's Barrett, Ricky Barrett. We been talking amongst ourselves and figured we'd try to be team players. From what I saw coming out of Knoxville, the ones who didn't want to be team players went down pretty fast."

I nodded and hit the button to raise the garage doors. The building had been intended for a lot more cars than we brought in.

"Let's get 'em inside and take a look at what we got to work with. We got a race to win."

We hope that you enjoyed this title and look forward to many more to come. Please, leave us a review! Reviews matter to all of our authors.

Check out the latest in the Car Warriors: Autoduel Chronicle fiction series.
https://threeravenspublishing.com/car-warriors-autoduel-chronicles/

And don't forget to check out
the latest edition of **Car Wars**

http://www.sjgames.com/car-wars/

Or the other amazing titles from
Steve Jackson Games

STEVE
JACKSON
GAMES

AVAILABLE ON AMAZON
JOINT TASK FORCE 13
HOLDING THE LINE
BETWEEN HEAVEN AND HELL
13

B.E.N.T.
BIOLOGIC   ENHANCED   NASCENT   TALENT

STARFLIGHT

IT CAME FROM THE
TRAILER PARK

You can also keep up to date with our latest release announcements on <u>Scifi.radio</u> and get some of the best fandom programing on the planet.

Scifi for your Wifi

And don't forget to check out our other Sponsors and Affiliates

A southern Appalachian jewel for craft beer lovers, Buck Bald Brewing offers something for everyone.
To discover more visit us at buckbaldbrewing.com

Revolution X is a testament to the power of collaboration, blending four unique styles into a cohesive, revolutionary sound. When these four individuals unite, the result is nothing short of musical Revolution!

Would you like to learn how to write and market your own titles? The following affiliates links might be helpful.

Three Ravens Publishing is also a proud supporter of the Shepherd's Men and their mission to help veterans.

Comprised of active or retired servicemen and civilian volunteers, Shepherd's Men enthusiastically raises awareness and funds for the SHARE Military Initiative (SHARE) at Shepherd Center in Atlanta, GA.

This nationally renowned program focuses on assessment and treatment for American military veterans who have sustained mild to moderate Traumatic Brain Injury (TBI) and Post-Traumatic Stress Disorder (PTSD) during post-9/11 service.

Find out more at: https://www.shepherdsmen.com/

www.ingramcontent.com/pod-product-compliance
Lightning Source LLC
Chambersburg PA
CBHW032014310726